I0620906

KAYLA WREN

Bonus Study

BLACK CHERRY

PUBLISHING

First published by Black Cherry Publishing 2021

Copyright © 2021 by Kayla Wren

All rights reserved. No part of this publication may be reproduced, stored or transmitted in any form or by any means, electronic, mechanical, photocopying, recording, scanning, or otherwise without written permission from the publisher. It is illegal to copy this book, post it to a website, or distribute it by any other means without permission.

This novel is entirely a work of fiction. The names, characters and incidents portrayed in it are the work of the author's imagination. Any resemblance to actual persons, living or dead, events or localities is entirely coincidental.

Kayla Wren asserts the moral right to be identified as the author of this work.

First edition

ISBN: 978-1-914242-36-6

Cover art by Black Cherry Book Covers

This book was professionally typeset on Reedsy.
Find out more at reedsy.com

Contents

Keep in touch with Kayla!

Want to hear about new releases, sales, bonus content and other cool stuff? Sign up for Kayla's newsletter at www.kaylawrenauthor.com/newsletter!

1

Prologue

I stride down the hallway, already annoyed with myself. The walls are painted sage green, and sconces cast pools of warm light over the floorboards. I'm out of place, as always. Too big, too bulky, too loud. Normally I wouldn't give a shit—would relish that constant *fuck you* that my presence brings—but tonight, I wince as the floorboards creak under my weight.

I'm still not sure. Not sold on being here. I received the invitation a few days ago—a peace offering from the man who used to be one of my closest friends. I tossed my phone on the desk, Gideon's text still lit up on the screen, and tipped my head back and groaned.

How? How am I supposed to be okay with this?

He was a professor. Like me. Put in charge of students and given a duty of care.

Fraser—goddamn Fraser—has put it behind him. Has gone for dinner with Gideon and his student girlfriend. He says they're sweet together, if a little sickening. So in-your-face in love that their rough start doesn't seem to matter.

It matters to me. When I think of my students…

God.

How could he?

My feet carry me down the long hallway, and I tug at the collar of my shirt. A bottle of wine dangles from my other hand—my own peace offering. The gesture that will heal this rift between us.

I come to a stop outside Gideon's apartment. Inside, the faint strains of music and laughter echo through the wood. Someone calls through the rooms, and another voice answers. There's no hint of shame to this night—no attempt to hide away their relationship. They've invited all their friends over, refusing to hide away, and if I walk through this door I'm complicit. I'm telling Gideon and the world that it's okay; that he never crossed an uncrossable line.

Shame coils around my throat and squeezes. In the dark recesses of my mind, I'm well acquainted with that line. Left to my own unforgivable thoughts, I've crossed it time and time again.

Shit. Haven't I done enough?

A feminine giggle sounds on the other side of the door, and I turn on my heel without a word. The wine bottle swings in my grip as I stride away, my chest already loosening. I breathe better as I pound down the apartment building steps, spilling out into the cold January wind. It slaps my cheeks and tugs at my short hair. It spills freezing, minty air down my collar.

A run. That's what I need. A pounding, grueling run through the city streets, or a torture session in the campus boxing gym.

Less thinking, more sweating.

Yeah.

I need to grind these shameful thoughts out of my body.

Sweat the bitterness from my pores. And find something—anything—to distract myself from the sweet face that flashes across my mind. Lilac hair and thick-framed glasses.

No. I slam those thoughts of her away.

I'm not Gideon Warwick.

I will never cross that line.

2

Chapter One

I knew when I picked Sports Science that I'd be outnumbered by guys. You don't have to be a genius to predict it: all you have to do is glance around the nearest gym or sports bar. Mom warned me I was going into a male-dominated field on the day she dropped me at the airport in Phoenix, but she said it with a wicked glint in her eye. And when she hugged me goodbye, she whispered, "Keeley? My sweet girl. Give 'em hell."

A smile plays over my lips as I barrel into the Sports Science department building, raindrops clinging to my light purple hair.

My mom needn't worry. I intend to.

It's early—too early for ninety percent of the student population to be awake. My thighs are hot and aching already from my morning workout, and the thermos clutched in my hand is ready to see me through.

New semester. New module; new challenges.

Let's do this.

Apparently not everyone is so bouncy first thing on a January morning. When I push through the doors into the lecture hall, the handful of students that are already here are slumped over the desks like wounded soldiers. I give them bright smiles anyway, peering through the spots of rain on my glasses.

One guy rolls his eyes.

Whatever. No need to be rude.

My favorite seat in this ancient lecture hall is right in the front row. After three years' worth of experimentation, I've found it has the squishiest padding and the best acoustics to hear the professor. I march straight over, ignoring the grumbles from other students.

They think I'm a know-it-all. Some kind of cheat, just because I'm a girl and I beat their asses in every class.

I don't cheat. I study. I train. I work harder than these idiots even know how to.

That's not a very generous thought. I force myself to smile at my nearest neighbor as I slide into my seat. He huffs, shaking his head and digging out his phone.

Fine. I tried.

The ancient heater bolted to the far wall clunks and rattles to life. It wheezes out hot, stale air, swirling dust around the small room, and I tug my sweatshirt up over my nose.

The Sports Science lecture halls are the worst on campus. I get it—the department wants to spend all its budget on cool gadgets and equipment. Believe me, I'm with them. There's an altitude simulator that I'm dying to get my hands on.

"Jesus Christ," the nearest guy mutters, dropping his phone onto the desk. He drops his head onto his folded arms and swiftly falls asleep.

Yeah. It's kind of hard to concentrate when the room gets all hot and muggy.

It's even worse when the professor walks in.

Professor Beckett Hale is the biggest name in the Sports Science department. He's published groundbreaking research, yes, but he's also coached elite athletes to gold medals and broken records. He eats, sleeps and breathes sport, from his short dark hair all the way down to his beat up running shoes.

I stifle a smile, peering at the cracked, worn leather as he passes. For some reason, those beat up sneakers always make my chest warm. Has no one told this man he's a legend?

The rest of his clothes are understated, too. He's in navy blue sweatpants that cling to his muscled thighs, and a white t-shirt that stretches over his broad chest. Professor Hale doesn't even look up from his phone as he crosses the room. He scowls down at the screen, a Llewellyn College sweatshirt gripped in his other hand.

"Alright." His clear, deep voice bounces around the hot room. Half the students still aren't even here, but Professor Hale doesn't seem to give a shit. He flicks a glance around the empty seats, my cheeks flushing as he passes over me, then looks back at his phone, unbothered.

"Let's get out of here." He clicks the screen off and shoves it in his pocket. When he crosses his arms over his chest, his shoulder-to-waist ratio is freaking sinful. "No lecture slides today. We're gonna run. And it's gonna hurt."

A few groans sound in the back rows, but I can't help the grin stretching over my cheeks. Professor Hale glances at me again, his scowl snagging on the way I'm practically bouncing in my seat.

I can't help it. I don't care if I already worked out this morning; I love running.

The pounding of my feet against the sidewalk. The steady

thump of my heart; the swing of my arms as my hair streams out behind me.

It's freedom. It's flying. And I know before we've even stashed our bags and stood—I'm going to leave these guys in my dust.

* * *

"Class doesn't actually start for another five minutes."

My head barely reaches past Professor Hale's shoulder when I bounce over to walk beside him in the courtyard. That's saying something—I'm at least as tall as half the guys in this class. Tall and strong. No wonder they grumble when they see me coming.

"So?"

Man, he sounds pissy. Professor Hale is clearly not a morning person. I rummage in my sweatpants pocket, pulling out a cereal bar and offering it to him. He scowls harder when he sees it, shaking his head and muttering something under his breath.

"So, half the students aren't here yet." I stash the cereal bar back in my pocket. "They'll miss the lesson."

"They are getting a lesson, Keeley." Hey, when did he learn my name? I grow three inches, beaming at the side of his grumpy face. "They're learning to turn up early."

"Is that fair?" I nudge him with my elbow and he jerks away, alarmed. I keep my smile fixed in place so he doesn't see my gut sink. "They're paying to be here."

Professor Hale sighs, his long legs slowing to a halt. He checks his watch, face stony, then turns, cups his hands around his mouth and bellows.

"Sports Science seniors! Courtyard, now!"

7

A pigeon bursts out of a nearby tree. It careens into the sky, wings flapping like crazy, feathers drifting down to the paving stones. In the distance, the sound of footsteps pounding over the stone paths echoes across campus.

"See?" I shove my hands in my pockets to keep from nudging him again. "They want to be here."

Professor Hale says nothing. He watches the latecomers run to catch up, bags thumping against their backs, with a muscle twitching in his jaw.

"Maybe you should let them drop off their stuff—"

"Enough, Keeley." My shoulders slump. I back up, reaching for the tree beside the path and steadying myself while I stretch out my quads. Professor Hale watches me for a second, mouth twisted, then he turns on his heel and whistles for the crowd of runners.

It's piercing. A call to action. My heart begins a drumbeat in my chest. I shake out my arms.

We take off as one, Professor Hale in the lead, our sneakers pounding the courtyard. We jostle for position, the slower or just more patient runners dropping back while the big shots push for the front. There are two other girls in this class, one brunette and a redhead, but they're not even trying to match the boys. They run together at the back, talking quietly, and for a second loneliness squeezes my chest.

It doesn't matter. I'm running my own race. And I have Raine and Lucy back home.

A few of the cockier students practically nip at Professor Hale's heels, and I wait for him to bark out orders at them. Instead, he drops back. Moves to the side and lets one of the fastest guys take over. Professor Hale drifts back in the group until he's running at my pace, just a few students over.

8

A dip in the path makes me stumble, and I shake myself. What, am I gonna stare at my professor for this whole run? No way. I'm not here to work on my stupid crush. I'm here to learn. To win.

I pick up my pace, legs pumping easily beneath me. This is part of the challenge we've been set—we're pacing ourselves without all the details. How far are we going? What kind of terrain? Are we doing hills?

I glance over at Professor Hale. He winks.

Yeah. I figured. He told us as much, back in the classroom: We're gonna run. And it's gonna hurt.

I shake my head, smiling, and focus on the ground rising up to meet me. The January air slices my chest on its way into my lungs, and my blood pulses through my thighs.

I was made for this.

If they don't know it yet, they will soon.

* * *

We stagger back into the courtyard, wheezing for breath. One guy—one of the runners who pushed for the front—stumbles to the flowerbeds bordering the courtyard and throws up his breakfast. He clutches his knees as he bends over, his face flushed a bright, sweaty red.

Yeah. Pacing's a bitch at the best of times, and Professor Hale didn't give us any clues. Still, this guy should know better than to rush the starting line. I wrinkle my nose, mouth pursing in sympathy.

Sneakers thump against the paving stones as the rest of the group arrive one by one. Some of them aren't even sweaty, their faces bored and dry, while others are flushed and gasping.

I don't have to look in the nearest reflection. I know surer than I know my own name: I'm bright scarlet.

A stitch pulses in my side and I prop my hands on my hips, forcing my breathing to steady. I walk up and down, my heartbeat thundering in my ears as the final stragglers arrive. The other girls run past, offering me small smiles, and I manage a feeble wave, still too winded to speak.

Doesn't matter. I tip my head back, beaming up at the white wisps of cloud.

I won.

Professor Hale jogs in last, tailing a green-faced guy on the swim team. The professor looks completely unaffected—like he's been lounging in an armchair, not running for almost an hour. He catches my eye as he passes, eyebrow quirking, and for a second I try to picture what he sees.

Bedraggled purple hair. Flushed, sweaty cheeks. A heaving chest and trembling legs. I curse quietly, scrubbing my forehead with my sweatshirt sleeve.

It doesn't matter. I'm just a student to him, never mind my crush. That's all I'll ever be to Professor Hale: an over-eager girl.

I still want to tug my collar up to my eyebrows.

"Good work." The professor's voice echoes around the courtyard. His mouth twitches at the state of us—sucking in desperate breaths and leaning against stone walls and trees. "We're starting the semester as we mean to go on."

I bounce on the balls of my feet, my exhaustion forgotten. All the good classes are in this semester, and I've been dreaming of this for months. Advanced Physiology; the Psychology of Sport; research projects and class freaking trips. My hamstring twinges and I drop into a stretch, forcing myself to concentrate.

He recaps the lesson. Ties it back to training principles. And then says the words which send my heart sinking to the ground: *work in pairs.*

It's our first assignment of the semester. An important research project.

And we're working in pairs.

Look, I like people. I'm always happy to do group projects. But... a single partner? Half of these guys hate me for beating them all the time, and the others are indifferent. No one wants to partner me.

I wrap my arms around my waist as Professor Hale counts us off, digging my thumbs into my sweatshirt sleeves. At least he's giving us this small mercy—he's choosing our partners for us, saving me from the humiliation of being picked last like in middle school gym.

"Keeley." His brown eyes land on me, narrowing for a second. Then he points at the top guy in our class. "And Brandon."

Brandon groans, loud enough for everyone to hear. Professor Hale moves on, mouth tight, but it's no use pretending. We all heard. My cheeks flush impossibly redder, and I offer Brandon a small nod. He scuffs his sneaker on the paving stones, hands shoved in his pockets.

Yeah, I'm not thrilled either, buddy.

It's not fair. If I were a guy, they'd be tripping over themselves to pair up. To have my skills and hard work on their team. But because I have boobs, I'm the enemy. The girl who's denting everyone's precious egos.

I glare at the ground, eyes stinging. And when Brandon huffs and comes over at the end of class, asking for my number, I plug it into his phone without a word.

For once, I don't feel like killing them with kindness. I don't want to tease the professor or strike up a strained conversation with the other girls.

I type in my number, hand Brandon's phone back, and take off jogging back to the classroom. My legs are like jelly, but I don't care, and I push to go faster as I weave between the students spilling out of the buildings.

It doesn't matter. I tell myself so over and over, my breath hitching in my lungs.

I'll give 'em hell.

Chapter Two

I f I weren't that little shit Brandon's professor, I'd beat his ass into the flowerbeds. I paired him with Keeley because she's top of the class and he's second, and she deserves a good partner.

Turns out he's an ungrateful dumbass. I'll remember that.

I want to say something to her, to make this right, but she takes off as soon as class is done. My chest aches as I watch her leave, jogging across the courtyard like all these other idiots aren't still chucking up their food. One of the guys snickers, elbowing his friend, and I turn the force of my glare on them.

Assholes. They're too wrapped up in their fragile egos to appreciate true talent when they see it. And because Keeley isn't tiny and stick thin, because she's gorgeous in a different way—

I curse and stride away.

I can't think of her like that. She deserves so much more from her professor. I'm no better really than these other let-downs.

"Shit," I mutter as I walk. "Shit."

I wheel down the stone path toward the Student Wellness

Center, churned up flowerbeds lining either side. The day's barely started. I should go to my office and work on my next paper; I should plan lessons or go and train. But seeing her has spun me out. It always does. My strides eat up the path and the automatic door whooshes to the side.

The Wellness Center is a tragic building. It's worn and exhausted, but in an enjoyable way. The motivational posters peeling away from the waiting room walls are laughably bad—literally. Fraser chose the ones that made him cringe the most. And Maggie the receptionist is hapless but sweet, her tortoiseshell glasses too big for her face. They slide down her nose as I step inside, and she flaps a hand over her chest.

"Beckett! I didn't know you were coming!"

When she knows, Maggie puts on pearly pink lipstick. It's less awkward this way.

"Didn't want you to run and hide, Mags."

She gasps and titters, waving at me as I cross the lobby and head down the hall.

I've spent a lot of time in this building. More time than in my own office. I know the warren of corridors like the back of my hand, and I find my way to Fraser's office on autopilot.

I pause outside the door. No way am I going to burst in on some poor tortured soul trying to bare their heart. Fraser attracts them like butterflies to nectar—which makes sense, as a guidance counselor. But here I am, too. The burliest butterfly on campus.

It's silent behind the wood. I rap twice, hard. Amusement curls through Fraser's voice as he calls, "Come in, Beckett."

His grin drops when he sees my face.

"What happened?"

"Nothing." I throw myself into the spare chair, the metal legs

14

screaming under my bulk, and bury my face in my hands. "Just some little shit in my class."

Fraser snorts. "Don't you have access to a boxing gym? Kick his ass."

I peer between my fingers. "Is that the official advice?"

"Definitely. Violence is the answer."

"Some shrink you are."

Fraser levels me a look, his piercing blue eyes boring straight through me. It's the type of look that says: *cut the shit*. He's right, of course. I've burst in here, interrupting his work or his nap or whatever the hell he does, and now I'm being a dick. I hold my palms up in surrender.

"You're right. You're right. I'll kick his ass tomorrow."

"Glad to hear it. Now tell me why you're really here."

This is the problem with having a psychology professor for a friend. Even one who's kicking back as a guidance counselor. They psychoanalyze the shit out of you. I shrug, uncomfortable, suddenly wishing I'd stormed off to the coffee shop after class instead of here.

"Gideon was asking after you," Fraser says, watching me carefully. "He misses you, Beck."

I dig the heel of my palm into my eye. "Leave it, man."

"Maybe if you saw the two of them together—"

I launch to my feet, glaring at Fraser as he sits wide-eyed in his chair. With a growl, I start to pace his tiny office, my blood roaring in my ears.

"I'm not going to see them together. He's her professor! It's fucking wrong."

"He's not her professor anymore," Fraser says lightly. I toss him a scowl over my shoulder.

"She's still too young. You're the damn guidance counselor.

How can you be okay with this?" I reach the wall and spin around. I must look insane—like a bear at the zoo—but I can't sit still and have this conversation.

Not with Keeley's flushed cheeks and bright eyes still fresh in my mind.

I'm such a goddamn hypocrite.

"I'm not condoning it." Fraser sounds so tired. "But it's done now. It's over with. And he makes Lucy happy—he left his job for her. What else do you want from him?"

I want him to be better.

I want both of us to be better.

I want to be told how to resist this pull.

"I don't know," I admit, coming to a stop by his desk. I tug at the waxy leaves of a potted shrub and Fraser swats at me, annoyed. "Actually yeah, I do. I want answers. I want to know how he looks himself in the eye."

"For your own benefit?" Fraser asks, and I whip my head around to look at him. He smiles up at me, bland and innocent.

"No," I say slowly. "This has nothing to do with me."

Fraser hums and says nothing. I count to five so I don't punch a hole in the wall.

"I would never do what he did." My voice is shaking, I'm so fervent. "I'd never touch a student."

Fraser nods, rocking on his chair. "That's good. Very reassuring. I'd have to report you, after all."

I stride to the door, gripping the handle and glaring over my shoulder.

"You're a terrible shrink."

His laughter follows me down the corridor.

Chapter Three

By the time I get back to the apartment, my sweatshirt has seen better days. This morning's run, along with the way my body naturally runs hot whenever Professor Hale is near, then a full day of lectures... well, there's no way around it. I stink.

"Stay back, woman." I hold up a palm when Raine sidles out of the kitchen, a bowl of popcorn balanced against her chest. She raises an eyebrow, shoving a handful into her mouth. "I smell like week old laundry. You've been warned."

My backpack clatters to the floor and I kick off my sneakers, wincing at a blister on my heel.

"Noted," Raine murmurs around her mouthful. She watches me yank out my ponytail and fluff my hair with her head cocked.

I address the pile of shoes by the door. "Don't even think about it."

Raine huffs a laugh. "What?"

I wave a hand at her without looking. "I know what you're doing. You know. Your *thing*. Don't psychoanalyze me."

"I wouldn't dare."

"Good." I step over my backpack, further into the warmth of the apartment. The TV is on in the living room, the volume on low as an old sit com plays. One of Raine's sweaters is draped over the back of the sofa, while a stack of Lucy's sketchbooks teeters on the coffee table. Our holiday twinkle lights are still slung around the walls, and the scent of something spicy makes my stomach growl.

Home sweet home. The knot in my chest eases slightly.

"You do seem off, though," Raine says behind me, trailing me into the kitchen. A huge pot of curry simmers on the hob, steam rattling its lid. I tug the refrigerator open with a sigh, digging for the ingredients for a green smoothie. "If I guess right, will you tell me?"

I grunt, noncommittal, and slap a bag of spinach onto the counter top.

"Is it class-related?"

I shrug. I'm not stressed about college stuff. Not really.

"Are you worrying about your weight again?"

I snort, slicing an apple. "Wow, I hate this game."

"That's a no." Raine hops up onto the counter beside me, swinging her heels as she studies me. Her smooth brown forehead creases, her dark eyes troubled. "Is something really wrong?"

I chew on the inside of my cheek, scooping up my raw fruits and veggies and dumping them in the blender. The truth is, I'm not even sure. Ever since this morning, I've felt... off. Jangled up and skittish. Too big for my own skin.

"I've been paired up with an asshole for an assignment." That's not it, not exactly, but it's easier to tell Raine that much than to dig any deeper. "Brandon. He let everyone know he wasn't

18

pleased to partner me, loud and clear. Right in front of the professor."

Raine's legs still. She scowls into her bowl, like the popcorn kernels are to blame.

"Fucker," she mutters. Then, louder: "He's a jerk, Keeley. Assholes like that don't win in life."

I think of Brandon's wavy brown hair. His square chin and broad shoulders; the way girls laugh at his unfunny jokes and guys compete for his attention. The designer labels on his sports gear.

"Sometimes they do."

Raine snarls, stuffing a handful of popcorn into her mouth and crunching down like she's picturing Brandon's bones. She might be quiet, but Raine is fierce. Unbreakable. She would never let an ass like Brandon dent her confidence, and that more than anything raises my chin.

"I outran him, though," I tell her, just to see her smile. Sure enough, she smirks, her eyes crinkling at the corners. When she tosses her hands up, the bowl wobbles on her lap and a stray piece of popcorn flies across the room.

"See? That's why he's throwing a fit. You bruised his stupid ego."

"Must be pretty fragile," I muse, blending my smoothie and pouring it into a glass. I take a sip and wince.

Damn. I'm a runner, not a cook. I eye Raine's curry not-so-subtly, and she scoffs before hopping off the counter and digging out two bowls. When the apartment door opens and Lucy's voice floats through the rooms, Raine adds another bowl without missing a beat.

This is it. I force myself to take another gulp of smoothie, feeling the day's tension bleed from my body. The longer

I'm here—in the warmth and the delicious smells, with Raine and Lucy chattering beside me—the more the stresses of this morning melt away.

Who cares if Brandon's an asshole? I don't need to like him, and he certainly doesn't need to like me. We can work together, finish the assignment, and that's it. No big deal.

As for the other thing—the real reason my body's been flushed hot and clumsy for hours—well. It would sound so stupid if I say it out loud.

I'm not Lucy. I'm not tiny and doll-like, with guys tripping over their tongues when I walk past.

It doesn't matter if I'm all jumbled up over Professor Hale. He's never given me a second thought.

* * *

I wait until Lucy and Raine are comatose on the sofa after dinner before I traipse off to the bathroom. I swipe my towel and shower bag from my bedroom, wincing at the old socks scattered over my floorboards.

Tomorrow. I'll get my shit together tomorrow.

Tonight, I just want to stand under scalding hot water for twenty minutes, then collapse into bed.

Our shower is ancient and temperamental. You have to twist the knobs to the exact perfect angle—half an inch wrong, and all you get is an ice-cold dribble. I set the water running, tugging my stinky sweatshirt over my head with a groan. My sore muscles flex on my back, screaming at me to do my damn yoga, and I step under the spray with an ungodly whimper.

"Oh, yes, Jesus." I turn in a circle, the hot water beating against my back. This is the best part of working out—the delicious feeling of a burning hot shower afterwards. I shampoo my hair in a daze, scratching at my scalp, when a thought comes into my mind unbidden.

It's a good thought.

I hum, my eyelids fluttering closed, and I picture other fingers in my hair. His fingers.

Professor Hale's.

He's so big, so freaking burly, that he'd barely fit in this little cubicle with me. His shoulders would scrape on the tiles on one side and the glass on the other, and he'd have to crowd so close, we'd be touching. If I wanted to meet his eye, I'd have to tilt my head back for a change. I bite my lip, my eyes screwing tighter shut as I try to picture it.

Would his chest be hairy? Yes. Definitely. He's got that scruff on his chin and jaw, that incredible, thick kind of growth that only really masculine men can produce. Brandon could *never*.

My imagined version of Professor Hale gets kind of blurry below the waist, but that's okay. I know what his hands look like. I've stared at them often enough in class, watching him gesture to the lecture screens or demonstrate how to use a piece of equipment. He's got thick fingers, with squared knuckles, but they're graceful hands, too. He's not clumsy, just big, and agile with it.

Jeez. I squeeze my legs together, soaping my chest. The thought of his hands there, squeezing me, tweaking my nipples, makes static crackle through my brain. I gasp, mimicking the movements—touching myself how I wish he would touch me.

He'd feel so different. Bigger and rougher and better.

I slide my hands down my stomach.

For one ridiculous moment, embarrassment courses through me. Not for what I'm doing, but because here in my daydream, it feels so real. And if it were real, if Professor Hale crowded into the shower, he'd see all of me. My broad shoulders. My muscled thighs. My stomach that has never, ever, no matter how much I exercise, been flat.

I huff, annoyed. Really? I can't even touch myself without putting myself down? I scowl at the bathroom tiles, eyes still screwed shut, and start moving my hands again.

He'd like it, I decide, as though if I think it hard enough, I can will it into existence. Professor Hale would be so fucking attracted to me, he wouldn't know what to do with himself.

He'd knead my aching shoulder muscles. Press tender kisses on my stomach as he dropped to his knees. And he'd hum and stroke up my thick thighs before he buried that scratchy face between my legs.

I stifle a moan, leaning one shoulder against the cubicle wall as I work myself. Even knelt down, he'd be so freaking tall, the muscles flexing on his back as he ate me out. My legs shake as I picture it—digging my nails into those massive shoulders. Feeling his hot skin on me, against me, everywhere.

"Shit!" I squeak as I come, doubling over from the force of it. The last suds of shampoo drip down my wet hair, landing on my painted turquoise toes, and my breathing is ragged in the steam-filled shower.

I finish washing with trembling hands, the ache in my abdomen dulled but still not gone.

5

Chapter Four

Two weeks into the semester, I'm almost myself again. Almost.

There's still a weird hollowness where my friendship with Gideon was. I keep catching myself pulling out my phone to text him something funny, or pausing during conversations with Fraser to give our absent friend time to speak. Fraser gives me such a *look* when I do that, a look that says I'm full of shit, but I roll my eyes and keep talking until he lets it drop.

Screw Gideon. These are just growing pains. A natural part of losing a friend. And if the last couple of weeks have proved anything, it's that it is perfectly possible to keep away from students.

Even heartbreakingly cute ones like Keeley. Every time I see her, it's like a punch to the gut—and it has been for the last three years. If I can do it, he fucking could have.

She's been there the last two weeks, eager and early in all of my senior classes. She's always smiling, always pushing those glasses up her freckled nose or pushing her lilac hair out of her eyes. Keeley Smith has been sent to test me, and so far, I'm indomitable. Impervious to the heart-breaker in my front row. I keep my face carefully blank, never letting my eyes linger on her too long. To any outside observers, I am cool. Detached. Professional.

Inside, of course, I'm slamming my head against the wall. But these idiots don't know that, do they?

"Alright. Come here," I say to the biggest idiot of all, beckoning Brandon to the edge of the ice bath. The rest of the class crowds around, notebooks clutched in their hands as they scribble along with the lecture. Keeley's pen has one of those fuzzy feather thingies on the end, and every time I glimpse it, I get the bizarre urge to tickle her with it.

Brandon swaggers forward, throwing a cheeky grin over his shoulder. His hands are shoved in his pockets—no notebook for him—and his hair has been artfully tousled.

God, I hate this kid.

He's always been an annoying little gnat, but since he scoffed at Keeley like that in the first class, loud enough for everyone to hear...

Well. The ice bath isn't usually an interactive class.

"In you get," I say cheerfully, suddenly enjoying myself way too much for a rainy Tuesday morning. The sky is gray and gloomy through the department window, but songbirds might as well be tweeting as I bounce on my heels.

"Uh." Brandon laughs nervously, raking a hand through his hair. "I don't have other clothes."

I smile at him, shark-like. "Don't worry. There's the lost and found."

For a second, his eyes narrow. They flick between me and Keeley, darkening, and something tightens in my gut. My pulse thrums in my neck, my skin flushing hot, and I'm fucking *caught*—but then he shrugs, grinning to his audience and playing it up as he toes off his shoes. Always the performer.

"Jeez, coach." He shakes his head, still grinning as he lowers himself into the water. "There better be extra credit for this." Chunks of ice coat the surface, bobbing with his movements, and his white t-shirt goes see-through, sticking to his chest. One of the girls in the class giggles, elbowing her friend and whispering.

I risk a glance at Keeley, but she's frowning down at her notebook, reading over her notes.

Good girl.

"Not your coach right now," I remind Brandon as his teeth start to chatter. He's one of *those* kids. He thinks because he's on a college sports team, he walks on water. Can do no wrong.

He's gifted, sure. Annoyingly so. But it comes too easy to him. He's never had to earn anything. And if he wants special treatment, he's in the wrong room.

"Tell us about ice baths, Brandon. Once you hit all the points, you can get out."

Fraser would have an embolism if he saw this class right now. But hell, Sports Science always has a practical element. More often than not, we demonstrate the equipment and processes to help the students learn. And if I'm pushing my luck with this...

At least I'm reining my worst urges in.

Still, I send another student to fetch a towel. And I make sure to call on others for the rest of the class. Brandon brings out an ugly side of me, and I don't want to be that guy. Not in general, and especially not around Keeley.

At the end of the hour, I pull him aside and agree to his damn extra credit. Keeley catches my eye over his shoulder and gives me a soft smile. Like she can sense how much it galls me.

I clear my throat and focus on the smug ass-hat in front of me.

It's going to be a long semester.

* * *

My phone pings as I'm locking up my office for the weekend. Normally, I'd ignore it—there's nothing that can't wait until I'm back on the clock on Monday. But Keeley had some questions about the first assignment earlier, and a pathetic part of me hopes it might be her again. She always puts a ton of exclamation points in her emails, and she signs them 'K'. It's so damn cute.

The email stops me in my tracks. I stand in the middle of the hallway, disgruntled students muttering as they give me a wide berth. *Coaching opportunity... Atlantic Ocean row...*

Shit. Not now.

Not when Keeley only has until the summer left in college. Not that I'd do anything once she's left—she's still too good, too young for me. But I'm a selfish bastard, and if I only have a few more months of her presence, I don't want to miss a minute.

This email, though. If it gets out that I've turned down this chance—and it will—the department will freak. The whole reason they give me so much leeway, letting me teach whatever I want and ordering in crazy expensive equipment, is because I pull in the headlines.

I coach the best athletes in the world. Lead underdog teams to victory.

I'm their meal ticket.

I sigh, digging my thumbs into my eyes. There's no way

around it, but still I can't bring myself to type out a response. I stand there frozen like an idiot, the sky darkening outside the windows as street lamps flicker to life.

"Fuck it," I mutter at last, clicking my phone off and shoving it into my pocket. This is a tomorrow problem.

The Sports Science building is a warren, but there's a shortcut out to the parking lot through the department gym. It's always bustling with energy, even in the late evenings, with the college's various sports teams sneaking in to use the equipment. We've got shit the main campus gym could never afford, and the players like to think it gives them an edge.

It doesn't.

There's no substitute for hard work. Nothing like putting in the hours, sweating your dues.

I scan the gym automatically as I weave between the machines, my backpack slung over one shoulder. The lights are dim, with music pumping through the speakers, and the mirrors lining the walls reflect endless bodies and sets of pumping limbs.

There—my heart squeezes in my chest. A flash of lilac hair in the corner. Without thinking, I alter course, heading toward the exit nearest Keeley instead.

I'm just gonna walk past. Maybe say hi. But when I catch a glimpse of her face, I stop dead.

She's red-faced. Blotchy and tear-stained, and not from a good workout. She's fucking distraught. She's standing by a treadmill, fixing electrodes to her chest above her tank top, her hair falling into her eyes. She keeps stopping to wipe her face on her sleeve.

I'm moving again before I can think straight. I stride up beside her, tossing my backpack down like it's on fire.

"What happened?"

27

Keeley flinches, ducking her head when she sees it's me. I don't blame her. I sound insane. My voice is low and thrumming with violence, and my fists are clenched so tight my knuckles have turned white.

"Nothing happened," she murmurs, like I'm a blind man. Like I don't know her moods better than my own. "I stubbed my toe."

"Bullshit." Keeley glances up at me, alarmed, and I step closer. She backs up against the machine, her mouth parting slightly. "Something happened. Tell me about it. Tell me so I can fix it."

She frowns up at me, confused, and why wouldn't she be? This isn't how her professor should act. The reflection of us in the mirror says it all: a young, upset student and her surly, overbearing professor making her uncomfortable. I suck in a deep breath, forcing my shoulders to relax, and back up a step. The smile I plaster over my face is bland and professional.

"Is it course-related?"

Keeley's eyes drop. She shrugs one shoulder, turning back to the treadmill and pushing the buttons. The belt thrums to life, rattling as it picks up speed.

I try again. "Is it one of the assignments?"

She shrugs both shoulders this time. I'm getting closer.

"Keeley." I place my hands on her shoulders and turn her to face me. "Help me out here. I can't—I can't teach you properly if I don't know the problem."

She frowns down at our feet, bitterness etched on her face, and it's such an alien expression on her that my chest aches. Keeley Smith is a ball of sunshine. She's laughter and teasing; hard work and a happy outlook.

This girl is tired. Defeated. And since she's not going to offer up any answers, I peer over her shoulder and scan her set up.

The electrodes on her chest and her open notebook balanced on the treadmill tickle my memory, and I squeeze her shoulders without thinking.

"It's the paired assignment, isn't it?" I drop my hands, turning to glare around the gym. "Where's Brandon?" Whatever he's said to her, I'll kill the little shit.

Keeley's laugh is strangled.

"How should I know? He won't answer his damn phone." She clams up again, biting her lip. I close my eyes for a second, pulse thundering in my ears. The assignment is due in three days. Even if he turned up right this second and they both worked flat out, they'd struggle to get it done.

"He ditched you?"

Keeley breathes in hard through her nose, then blows it out and sets her shoulders back. In front of my eyes, she transforms from bitter and sad to determined. Glorious. She swipes at her face with her hoodie sleeve again, and when she looks at me again, her eyes are dry.

"It's fine, professor. I've got this."

Hell yeah, she does. I know that. But the point is, she shouldn't have to.

"Use me," I blurt. "For your experiment. You need someone to study, right? You can use me."

Gideon's face flashes across my mind. His words from last semester, whispered with so much shame: *I couldn't keep away.* I open my mouth to take back my reckless offer, to give an extension or something instead, but Keeley lights up. She smiles at me with so much raw relief, it takes my breath away.

"Really? Oh my god. That would be perfect. Seriously?"

I nod, inwardly cursing myself to hell. Keeley tears the electrodes off her chest, beaming. I move to pick them up,

29

to fasten them to my chest instead, but she waves me off.

"Forget those. I was desperate. That experiment sucks. Now that I have you, I can do way better."

Apprehension slides down my spine. "What do you have planned?"

Keeley bends down and scoops up both our backpacks, handing mine to me with a grin.

"Have you ever run in altitude, professor?"

Ah, shit.

6

Chapter Five

I don't know what makes me giddier: finally getting to use the hypoxic chamber, or bouncing down the hallway with Professor Hale at my side.

Seriously. The man is a great teacher, but he usually can't get away from me quick enough. Sometimes, when he ducks away from me after class, I get this horrible knot in my stomach because I'm so sure he can sense my feelings. Like my silly student crush is written all over my face, and he doesn't want to deal with it. Just wants to run away.

He's not running away from me now.

Professor Beckett Hale, demigod of the Sports Science department, just gave up whatever cool, sexy Friday night plans he must surely have had to help out with my assignment. It shouldn't be a plot twist—he's one of the best teachers on campus. Dedicated and patient.

I still have to bite my cheeks to keep from grinning. We walk together through the department hallways, falling naturally into step, and I find myself chattering at a hundred miles an hour out of nerves.

I tell him about my other classes.

About the apartment I share off campus with Lucy and Raine.

About my dreams for life after college.

I rant on and on, a spouting fire hydrant of chatter, and Professor Hale keeps stride with me the whole time. He nods and hums, asking calm questions when I stop for breath. Questions like my favorite sports and what hobbies I enjoy. The man deserves a medal—he can't truly be interested in this crap, but he's too honorable to tell me to quit yacking.

God. He's so awesome. This night is going to ruin me.

Especially since the sky is inky black through the hallway windows, and the classrooms we walk past are shadowed and empty. Every step we take deeper into the department warren is a step away from the rest of the world, and there's suddenly something so freaking intimate about being alone together in the dark corridors.

Rein it in, I tell myself sternly, blowing strands of hair off my flushed cheeks. My sneakers squeak with every step, and I focus on that sound instead of the silence wrapping around us.

The sounds of the gym fade. The shouts of other students, the clang of weights and the pumping music—they melt away until there's only the squeak of my shoes and the gentle rasp of our shared breaths.

"On your left."

I clatter to a halt, my backpack thumping against my hip. I was so focused on not being a pervy weirdo that I nearly marched right past the door to the chamber. Professor Hale digs a bunch of keys out of his back pocket, his face inscrutable as he flicks through them for the right one.

"You don't have to do this," I blurt out. The regret is clear in the tense set to his shoulders, in his clenched jaw. He frowns at me, sliding the key into the lock.

"I said I would, Keeley." He pushes the door open. "We're not all unreliable little pricks."

I snort as he leads the way inside, flicking the lights on. The chamber itself is like a room within a room—an air-locked cupboard with a treadmill inside and a big window. By controlling the oxygen content, we can mimic the air conditions of high altitudes and improve athletes' stamina.

It's awesome.

I drop my backpack on the fuzzy gray carpet and wander over to the controls. I've wanted to get my hands on this bad boy for months, but students hardly ever get permission.

"Brandon's going to freak when he finds out he missed this."

Professor Hale's voice is ice cold. "Too fucking bad."

I can't help the teasing smile I throw over my shoulder. He's got his arms crossed over that burly chest, his expression thunderous as he scowls at the controls.

"You're not supposed to curse around me."

Professor Hale sighs. "There are a lot of things I'm not supposed to do, Keeley."

An ache pulses hot and needy between my legs. I clear my throat, trying to sneakily squeeze my thighs together as I press the buttons.

"Like help out with assignments?"

"Something like that."

I wait for him to explain, to say more, but he's silent. A brick wall. A few times, he reaches around me to press the right buttons, my skin shivering at the almost-touch, but then he draws his hand back and leaves me in a gooey, tongue-tied puddle.

I screw my eyes shut. Give myself a little shake. And when I

33

set the program running, turning around to give him a thumbs up, I'm almost a normal human again.

"Ready to suffer for science?"

Professor Hale rolls his eyes, mouth twitching. If I ever made him laugh one day, really laugh, with a booming sound and his head tossed back…

I'd never recover.

"Yes, Keeley." Maybe it's wishful thinking, but I swear he winks at me as he tugs off his Llewellyn College sweatshirt. "I was born to suffer."

* * *

It's humiliating, but I have to remind myself more than once that I'm here to do an experiment, not to ogle my professor. It shouldn't be surprising that he's stripped to his bare chest in order to run—it's baking hot in here, thanks to the ancient heaters, and who wants to run in layers anyway? Hell, I'd run without a shirt every time if my boobs wouldn't take someone's eye out.

Still. The sight of that muscled chest shining with sweat, dusted with dark hair just like I'd imagined in the shower—

My pencil clatters to the floor, and I duck to snatch it up, cheeks flaming. Professor Hale keeps running, his legs pounding away at the treadmill through the glass. A bead of sweat slides down the center of his chest, trickling down his rippling abs until it soaks into the top of his sweatpants.

Jesus, Mary and Joseph.

Have I always been such a horn dog?

My stopwatch beeps, and I wave at him to take a break. He hops off the treadmill, strolling to the side of the chamber to measure his heart rate.

He doesn't look tired. He doesn't even look bothered.

He looks like a whole damn meal.

"Shut the hell up," I mutter to myself, turning my back so I can force myself to concentrate. I record the latest data, checking and double checking everything we've done so far. The clock on the wall shows it's long past 9pm—we've been here for hours, tucked away together in the depths of the department. I keep pinching myself to make sure it's not some lucid dream, but the musty smell of the carpet is a clue. This is really happening.

Professor Hale hasn't told me to hurry up once. The only time he looks pissed off is when I bring up Brandon. I almost feel kind of bad about my deadbeat partner—there's no way he can convince the professor he helped with the assignment now.

Almost.

The jerk should have answered his phone.

A sly voice in my head whispers that I should drag this out. Keep the professor here as long as I humanly can, committing his delicious chest to memory. Maybe if he spent enough time with me one-on-one, away from the other students, he'd start to see me as a person. A *woman.* Someone he could desire.

No. I slam my notebook closed, forcing a smile as Professor Hale lets himself out of the chamber and rejoins me in the main room.

"All done?" he asks, his chest heaving but his deep voice steady.

I nod. "Yep. Torture session over. Thank you so much for this."

"It's nothing," he mutters gruffly, tugging his t-shirt and sweatshirt over his head in one. It musses his short hair up, makes it stick in all directions, and I grip my notebook tighter

35

to keep from smoothing it down.

"Seriously." I can't seem to stop babbling, nerves making my chest tight. He watches me closely, dark eyes unreadable. "You're a life saver. I've been freaking out about this assignment."

"You could have come to me." He shoulders his bag, jaw tight. "Rather than let it get out of hand." And, yeah—I just ruined his Friday night. I should have asked for an extension days ago.

"Right. Sorry." I drop into a crouch, hiding behind my hair as I stuff my things into my bag. He makes a noise somewhere above my head, but when I straighten up his face is blank.

It's stupid. So freaking stupid. But the quiet hours spent together in the dark must have gone to my head. I want to thank this sweet, grumpy man.

I move on instinct, wrapping my arms around his waist and pressing my cheek to his chest. I can feel the thump of his heart, still racing from his run; I can smell his deodorant and fresh sweat. For a split second, my eyes drift closed and my breathing finally calms.

"Keeley." He pushes me away by the shoulders, a fierce scowl etched over his face. My stomach flips at his expression, at the censure in that one word, and bile rises in the back of my throat.

"Sorry," I whisper, swallowing hard. "I—god. I'm sorry."

His scowl stays fixed as I dart out of the classroom, twisting the hem of my sweatshirt as I wait for him to lock up. Our walk back through the halls is the exact opposite of earlier: tense and silent. My stomach sinks more with every squeaking step of my shoe, and by the time the faint strains of gym music drift down the hall, there's a sharp lump in my throat.

"Thank you," I whisper when we reach the exit. My throat is

too tight to speak any louder. "Goodnight, professor."

I don't wait for him to reply. Nor do I dare look at that scowl again. I turn on my heel and plunge into the darkness of the parking lot, absurdly grateful for the icy slap of the February wind. My cheeks burn so hot, I will never be pale again, and I gulp back humiliated tears as I start to jog.

What the hell was I thinking?

God. He must think I'm truly pathetic. A student crushing on her professor—such a cliche. And now it's not even a secret anymore, now he *knows*. I want to howl at the damn moon.

I pick up speed, my sneakers thundering over the stone path as I wind my way across campus. My muscles are cold and stiff, but I push to go faster, pumping my arms. My heart is pounding so hard in my chest, it feels like it could burst straight out of my rib cage.

I run so fast, I'm two steps from flying. Tears streak cold across my cheeks, freezing against my hot skin, and there's nothing but the drumbeat of my footsteps and the churning in my stomach. I burst off campus, wheeling into the city streets, and let out a bark of laughter as a businessman lurches out of my path, alarmed.

Fuck. How ridiculous.

A reluctant grin stretches my cheeks, even as the tears keep streaming.

What was I thinking?

Chapter Six

She's avoiding me. Keeley. Every time she sees me coming near on campus, she ducks her purple head and walks the other way.

I could handle that. Hell, it's probably for the best—my control around her is wearing thin, and god knows what I'd do or say if we were alone again. But it's affecting her education. Her future career.

I scan the sheet of paper for the fifth time, one hand gripping the edge of my desk. Disbelief and regret war inside me, and I clench my jaw so hard my teeth hurt.

She didn't apply. Keeley didn't submit her name for the class ski trip—the biggest event of the semester, and one she's been excited about for months. I know, because she's told me, oh, about a hundred times, her footsteps bouncing along the department's hallways and her ponytail swinging. You'd think I'd get bored of hearing about it, but her enthusiasm is contagious. Even I was looking forward to it after a while—or looking forward to seeing her happy, anyway.

She hasn't even applied.

Because of me.

Shit.

This is why I wanted to keep my distance. Nothing has even happened between us, and already she's worse off. Did I really hurt her feelings that badly? Surely she knows why she can't hug me like that.

"God help me," I mutter, tossing the list of names onto my desk and scrubbing both hands down my face. The paper lands on a rare tidy patch of my desk, the rest of the surface a riot of printed out essays and office supplies. A framed photo of my siblings, all overgrown adults crammed together into my mom's tiny kitchen, leans lopsided against my full in-tray. Somewhere in the wreckage, a pile of paper clips slide off the desk and patter against the carpet.

I'm not usually this bad. A bit chaotic, sure, but not outright messy. The framed diplomas and photos of gold medal teams lining the walls—those aren't the work of a slob. My equipment is always in mint condition, and my training schedules are precise. Exacting.

Yet here I am, a grown man in his thirties, hiding in the bomb site of his office and obsessing over a female student's hurt feelings.

Shit.

I bring up the class schedules on my monitor before I can think better of it, my fingers thundering over the keyboard. This isn't... unreasonable. It's a normal, respectable concern. She's my student, and I'm asking about her educational choices.

Math. She's on the other side of campus, taking one of the required classes. The lecturer is a name I don't recognize, and after the smallest pause, I bring up his head shot with a surge of self loathing.

Professor Walker. He's handsome, because of course he is. All blond hair and blue eyes. God fucking damn it.

"Professor?" There's a knock against my door frame. I glance up, mood already sour.

"What is it, Brandon?"

His cocky grin dims, but only a fraction. Then he rallies, pushing off the door frame, and saunters into my office. A stapled paper dangles loosely from one hand—his paired assignment. I recognize the big zero in red.

"I think there's been some misunderstanding, coach." He raises his paper, waving it around with a wide smile like we're in on some kind of joke. Like I'm pranking him because we're just that close. "You failed me on the paired assignment."

I lean back in my chair until it creaks. Oh, yeah. On second thought, I'm glad Brandon's here. I'm going to enjoy this.

"I did. What misunderstanding are you referring to?"

He laughs, loud and brittle.

"Well, you didn't fail Keeley. She was my partner. It's the same assignment. She got top f—top grades."

I hum and nod, like it's a fair observation. Jesus, I can't believe this kid. What kind of silver spoon existence has he lived this far to think he'd get away with this shit? He's shameless. Even if it weren't Keeley he'd screwed over, I'd still enjoy raking him over the coals.

My eyes flick to the photo of my siblings. To my mom's worn kitchen, with her ancient appliances. To the hardest working group of people I know.

Brandon is barking up the wrong damn tree.

"Which parts did you work on?" I'll play along. It's better than charging off to the Math building like a fool. Brandon grins, relieved and flicks through the pages, reading out sections at

40

random. I nod and scribble down notes on scrap paper, like I'm listening, like I care. Then I pause and glance up, pen hovering. "Did you conduct the experiment together? Or just write it up?"

He'll fail either way, but I want to know exactly how much of a liar he is.

"We did the whole thing together," he says at once. Then he leans in, one eye squinting shut, like he doesn't want to tell me this. "Strictly speaking, I did more than Keeley. She's enthusiastic, you know, but kind of a liability."

My heart thumps so hard in my chest, it's going to bruise. I can hear my breath saw in and out of my lungs.

"Coach?"

I give myself a shake, and everything fades back in.

I'm done with this. I got what I needed—absolute proof that Brandon is a jackass.

"The zero stands," I rasp. Brandon frowns, darting a glance down at my notes like he'll find something there. Some kind of lifeline. "You're on academic probation and there is a note in your file. Any further instances of cheating, and you'll be removed from the program. And you're benched from the football team for the rest of the semester."

"You can't—"

"I can and I have," I snarl, pushing to my feet. My fists rest on my desk, and I glare down at the younger man. If we weren't professor and student, I'd drag him out to the quad and kick his ass. He's lucky I still don't.

"It's her word against mine!" Spots of color glow high on his cheeks. Brandon's eyes are bright. Manic. "Just because you clearly want to fuck her, doesn't mean you can take sides—"

"Watch yourself," I say, low and deadly. I'm not getting in a shouting match with a hysterical child. "Keeley didn't rat you out, *I* helped with her assignment. Filled in when you left her hanging. So are you going to tell me you were there too, and I just didn't see you? Is that what you're trying to say?"

He opens his mouth and closes it again. He's caught out and he knows it.

I bet he's never faced a consequence in his whole privileged life. Well, I'm delighted to do the honors.

"Next assignment is due in two weeks." I clap him on the shoulder as I round the desk. He sways under my palm. "You can still pass the class if you ace all the rest. Better get studying, Brandon."

* * *

"I had an interesting day."

I find Keeley after the afternoon's classes end, working her lifeguard shift at the campus pool. I know entirely too much about Keeley's movements—where she works, what classes she goes to, where she likes to study. I haven't stalked her—she told me about it all herself, back when she told me things.

I just remembered. Committed every word to memory. It would be sad, if it weren't so dangerous. A constant temptation.

She jumps at the sound of my voice and looks down from the raised chair. She's sitting on what I always thought of as the lifeguards' throne, keeping an eye on the kids in the pool. Swimming lessons are underway, the surface of the water roiling like the pool is full of piranhas, floats flying left and right.

Her eyes widen when she sees me, then she jerks her head around to stare at the water.

42

Can't blame her. Those kids look lethal. But she's been avoiding my gaze for over a week. I can't stand it any longer.

"That's nice," she murmurs, forehead creasing in confusion. "Um. What was good about it?"

God, she's cute. I stroll around to stand in front of the chair. She can still see over my shoulder, but now her gaze keeps flicking down.

Better. I want her eyes on me.

"I didn't say it was good. I said it was interesting." My mouth quirks as her frown deepens. "I had a little visit from Brandon."

Keeley rolls her eyes, and I can't help my wide grin. Ninety percent of the time, she's sweetness and light. I love that ten percent when she gets a bit savage.

"What did he want?" she sighs. "I told him you wouldn't believe that he helped with that assignment. I did warn him."

"But you gave him a copy anyway."

Keeley shrugs, her smile devious as she watches a kid belly flop in the deep end.

"I figured he could dig his own grave."

I've missed this. The thought slams into me—I've missed chatting with her. Hearing her opinions; telling her about my day. It's not like we talk often, exactly, but before the hug, we'd fill the silence as we walked through the halls.

Now she won't even walk with me. She doesn't seek me out like she did before.

"There was another surprise," I say softly. I wait until she looks at me again before I speak. Her hair hangs in two braids on her shoulders, and her lifeguard's whistle dangles against her red polo shirt.

My face is level with her waist. I try not to think about that. About the... possibilities the lifeguards' chair brings.

43

"I got the list of names for the ski trip. You weren't on it."

She pauses, then shrugs one shoulder.

"I changed my mind about going."

"You've been excited for months."

"Well, not anymore."

"Because of me?" It's a risky question, skirting dangerously close to all the *stuff* that's unsaid between us. To everything we cannot say. But I have to know. Because if she just doesn't feel like going, fine. But if she's missing out on the trip she's dreamed about for months because of me, because of one stupid hug—

Keeley wets her lips. She darts a nervous glance down at me.

It's all the answer I need. I ball my hands into fists and shove them in my pockets to keep from reaching for her. I stand out like a sore thumb in this sweltering room, in my sweatpants and sneakers and t-shirt.

Keeley's legs are bare. So are her feet. It's so intimate, I want to dunk my head in the pool.

"Please apply."

She chews on her lip.

"Keeley. Don't miss out on this because of me. It was one tiny mistake. One moment of awkwardness. Come on, you'll regret it."

She lets out a sigh and meets my eyes. Her whisper is so quiet, it's nearly lost in the shouts and splashes echoing off the tiles.

"I didn't think you'd want me there."

My laugh is bitter. She flinches, but it's not aimed at her.

"Keeley." I step forward. I'm close, too close, and everyone can see but I can't bring myself to care. "That's the problem. I always want you there." She blinks at me, surprised, but I keep talking. I need to cover that little confession, bury it in other words. "Besides, when will you get a chance like this again?" I step back, jaw tight. "You're from Phoenix, right?" As if I didn't know. As if I didn't remember every detail. "Not much snow in Phoenix."

She nods slowly. A shy smile tugs her mouth.

"I do want to try skiing. I've never done it before."

"Atta girl." I lock her down before she can change her mind. "I'll add your name to the list."

"Don't I need to apply—"

I wave a hand. "What, am I going to turn down our best student? You're going."

With me. To a ski resort. Away from this campus, these classes, everything. *There will be other students*, I remind myself sternly. Nothing will change.

Maybe not. But a weight still lifts off my shoulders.

8

Chapter Seven

The bus idles at the sidewalk, the rumbling engine the only sound in the still dawn campus. Its dark windows are fogged from the cold, and steam spills out of the exhaust and billows towards the sky.

There are no clouds this morning. Not even a wisp. Just a cold, clear sky the color of spearmint, and frost crunching on the grass as I cross the quad.

I hitch my backpack higher on my shoulders and beam at a nearby pigeon.

This is it. The trip I've been dying to go on.

The ski trip. With Professor Hale.

A line of yawning students curls around the edge of the bus, overstuffed bags sliding off their shoulders. They're all bundled up in parkas and ski jackets, a few designer beanies showing who's skied before. I stride to the end of the line, bouncing bright and cheery, but I don't chat to anyone else.

They're not morning people, as a rule. I learned that the hard way.

Me, I woke up at 4am this morning, I was so freaking excited.

I sat bolt upright in bed like some Disney princess, sighing out of my frosted window at the silent city below. A scalding hot shower and a smoothie bowl breakfast only made me more excited, and now I can barely keep still in line.

"Morning, everyone." Professor Hale strides past, a duffel bag gripped in one hand and a ski jacket stretching over his wide shoulders. He's looking down at his phone again—he seems more distracted than usual these days—but he glances up when he reaches the door to the bus.

His warm eyes track along the line of students, and maybe it's wishful thinking, but I swear his mouth quirks up when he sees me. I flush hot under my winter layers, smiling shyly back, and I forget to breathe until Professor Hale looks away. He pulls out his list of names, checking us off one by one as we file onto the bus.

My heart speeds up as the line inches along. It'll be me any second. He'll look at me with those hazel eyes, and speak to me. Just to me.

"Keeley." I open my mouth to say hi as I stop in front of the bus door, but for the first time in my entire life, I'm tongue-tied. I give a little squeak and a nod, and his eyes crinkle in amusement.

Oh god. Oh god, oh god. I thought I had it bad before. But since Professor Hale sought me out in the campus pool and said those words, said he always wants me around—well, I'm screwed. My crush has become radioactive.

And thanks to that stupid hug, I know exactly what his hard chest feels like under my cheek. I know how he smells—like soap and pine.

"Stay out of trouble."

I swear he winks at me. I squeak again, cheeks flushing, and scurry up the steps to the bus. My backpack bounces off the seats as I shuffle down the aisle, but I only go a few steps before I realize the bus is full. Everyone is paired off or resolutely alone, caps pulled down as they nap against the windows. Brandon catches my eye, a spare seat beside him, and his face darkens.

No. No way.

I spin and stuff my bag into the luggage rack overhead, cheeks flaming as I lower into the second row.

"Teacher's pet," Brandon mutters, loud enough for everyone to hear. Muffled laughter echoes in the back.

The steps creak under Professor Hale's weight as he climbs in last, squeezing two headrests as he does a final count. His eyes narrow when he sees my flustered expression, but I shuffle lower in my seat.

Stupid Brandon.

The door hisses as it slides shut, then the bus rocks as it pulls away. Professor Hale takes one last look at me then slides into the row in front of mine. He stretches up to stow his duffel first, a strip of bare skin on his hip winking at me, then he sits and leans forward to talk to the driver.

Right.

I tug my scarf up over my nose, never mind the baking hot air blasting out of the heater by my legs. The seats are ancient and lumpy, their covers frayed, and I squirm to get comfy. It's a long drive into the mountains.

After twenty minutes, Professor Hale sits back, the back of his head coming close enough to touch. A sliver of his arm peeks between the seat and the bus window, and I could wriggle a finger through there. Test the softness of his sweatshirt.

I don't, obviously. I learned my lesson with that freaking hug, and anyway—I wouldn't dare. My mouth goes dry at the

48

thought.

The professor's phone buzzes, distracting me, and I try not to eavesdrop too badly as he answers. His voice is clipped but polite—a professional call, then. Something about a rowing team.

Professor Hale does a lot of consulting work. He works with the best. I'd give my left arm for a career like that.

He hangs up without ceremony, stuffing his phone in his pocket, then turns his head to gaze out the window. I look too, to see the city buildings flooding past, but instead I find a pair of hazel eyes reflected back at me.

Watching me. Not blinking. Not sliding away.

Staring.

I shiver, burrowing deeper into my scarf, but I keep my eyes glued on the glass. I bite my lip, the motion safely hidden by the wool, and squeeze my thighs together to relieve the sudden ache below my belly.

His eyes darken. Stare at me for another long moment, then he looks away. Leans forward to say something else to the driver.

I blow out a breath, slumping down in my seat. My heart is pounding like I just ran five miles.

It's going to be a long, long drive.

* * *

We get ten minutes to settle into our cabins, then we're heading out to the slopes. I tug my borrowed ski pants up my legs, sliding the suspenders over my shoulders, and take in my home for the next four days.

It's cozy. Well—small. Smaller than everyone else's cabin.

I'm apparently the only girl in the department who wanted to go skiing, so while the guys are sharing huge cabins in groups of four, I have this cute chalet. They might have private hot tubs and wood burners, but hey—I get this place all to myself.

Plus I'm sure I can sneak a dip in someone else's hot tub. Even if I have to wait until everyone is sleeping.

My cabin is one big room, apart from a little closet of a bathroom. The walls, floor and roof are all the same pine panels, and the bed has a worn but sweet hand-quilted bed spread. The windows look out over the mountains, at the ghostly washes of snow, and wind whistles past the glass.

"Hell yeah." I hop up onto my bed, crashing back and staring up at the ceiling. "This is the life."

The warm light from the bedside lamp tints the walls gold, and I sigh happily. Let myself wonder, just for a second, what Professor Hale's cabin is like.

He must have one of those nice ones, right? All to himself.

I wonder if he has a hot tub.

A heavy thump rattles my front door, a muffled voice yelling that we're heading out. I jump up, cramming my socked feet into snow boots and snatching my rented ski jacket on the way to the door.

Maybe I'll be great. An undiscovered prodigy. Maybe I'll be doing tricks and slaloms before the end of the day.

Anything could happen.

* * *

Damn, I suck at skiing.

Maybe I should mind. Maybe I should feel as embarrassed as all the guys seem to think I should. All but a few of them

50

zip around me, carving deep tracks in the snow, Brandon cutting the closest of all. I blink up at them from my permanent position on my ass, and stifle a laugh.

This is… not what I expected.

A few of the other guys have never skied before either, and they're right here with me, at the bottom of the slopes. We can only manage the tiniest incline, and the way we keep crashing into each other, we seem drunk out of our minds.

One guy's laughing with me. A nice guy called Oliver, who tried to help me up once then slipped and sent us both sprawling. We lay in a tangled pile of brightly colored limbs and crooked ski poles, until Professor Hale came over and peeled us apart.

"Sorry!" Oliver says cheerfully, sliding to one side and grabbing the professor to steady himself. I bite my lip at the older man's face. "It's harder than it looks."

"And it looks freaking impossible," I put in. I nod over both their shoulders and they turn to look, Professor Hale grabbing Oliver by the back of his jacket before he hits the deck.

The mountain is crowded. Peppered with people, some shuffling awkwardly like Oliver and me, while others do leaps and tricks and show off. There are swells and ramps cut into the snow, and a few brave skiers try their luck, soaring between the dotted trees.

Brandon shoots off the nearest ramp, tucking his legs beneath him, then lands as deft as a ballet dancer.

"Show off," I mutter as Brandon sends us a wave.

Professor Hale grunts.

Oliver hits the snow.

"We've got an instructor tomorrow." Professor Hale's cheeks are flushed around the edges of his beard when he turns to me. I want to boop the tip of his red nose. "He'll show you the basics better than I can."

"I can't wait," I tell him honestly, rocking on my skis. They shoot out from under me, and I plummet to the ground.

Two strong arms catch me easily, lifting me back up and holding me at arm's length. I grip his elbows, trying to put my skis down, but they're impossibly tangled, and after ten seconds of flailing, Oliver is howling with laughter.

"Shut up, Johnson," the professor barks, but he's grinning too as he finally puts me down. My skis are crossed, but he clicks my boots out of the frames and I stagger onto the snow.

"I'll get it." I wave a glove. "Olympics here we come, right Oliver?"

I'm just pleased that another student doesn't hate my guts, but Professor Hale's eyes narrow as they flick between us.

"Good," he mutters, then pushes off, sweeping easily over the snow as his dark jacket billows behind him.

"Damn," Oliver murmurs, watching the professor's sculpted silhouette. "Pour me some of that."

"Tell me about it," I say, then slam my mouth shut. But Oliver is not Brandon, and he only grins as he pushes to his feet, moving his skis gingerly into place.

"You good?" he asks, and I nod before watching him ski clumsily away. A kernel of hope forms in my chest.

Another Sports Science student doesn't hate me. And it seemed kind of like Professor Hale was...

Jealous.

I beam up at the clear blue sky, wobbling as I clip my boots back into my skis, then set them in position.

"Here we go," I mutter, pushing off.

My ass hits the snow.

9

Chapter Eight

T ake a bunch of students on a class trip, and the first thing they want to do is party.

I know that. Hell, I was a student once, about a thousand years ago.

Still, I can't help grumbling under my breath as I stalk around the cabins at 2am. Rowdy behavior, I can handle. Nasty hangovers? Sure. But they're being loud, and the nearest neighbors might complain.

Not to mention me. I train my body hard. Constantly push my own limits. I need my beauty sleep, damn it.

Surprise, surprise, it's Brandon's cabin that I end up thumping on. The pulsing music stops suddenly, and the stage whispers of drunk people float through the door.

Whatever. They're all of legal drinking age. I roll my eyes and call through the wood.

"Party all you want, but keep it down, alright? We get thrown off this mountain and you'll be sleeping on the bus."

The door opens a crack. A bleary-eyed student wedges his head in the gap.

"We're not partying," he slurs. "We're just hanging out."

"Sure you are. Just keep it down."

"Yes, coach."

I've never coached this kid in my life, but apparently that's what they all call me now. Another thing I should probably care about, but I just don't. As long as they do what they're told, that's as far as I'm interested.

I turn and stride down the cabin steps, the hard-packed snow crunching under my boots. After a pause, the door clicks shut and the music starts up again, but quieter.

Fine. They'll be the ones throwing up on the slopes. Sometimes you have to learn your lessons the hard way.

My cabin is set a ways apart from the others—thank god. It backs onto the tree line, the icy breeze whistling through the branches and rattling my windows. I suck in a deep lungful as I cut back across the pristine white wastes, the crisp scent of pine filling my nose. I'd been groggy when their music woke me, sluggish and pissed off, but this fresh, cold air scours me clean and wakes me up.

I can't help myself. I pause halfway back to my cabin, glancing at the small wooden chalet tagged on to the other buildings like an afterthought.

No lights. No crappy, pulsing music.

Is she partying with the others?

Or is she alone?

It doesn't matter. It *can't* matter, so I tear my eyes away and stomp back to my temporary base. The steps groan under my bulk, the wind moaning past my deck, and I almost miss it.

The gentle splash. The electric hum coming from the back of my cabin.

Alright, if Brandon's gatecrashed my hot tub as some kind of revenge, I'll drown the little shit. I don't care who his daddy is—I'll push his hundred-dollar-moisturizer complexion under the water and give him the swirly of his life.

"Don't fucking move," I boom out, storming around the deck corner, then slam to a halt.

Keeley sinks into the water with a squeak, her eyes wide as saucers. Steam curls around her body, off her wet skin, and her wet hair dances in the bubbles.

"Professor!"

... Alright.

My feet stutter back into action. I approach the hot tub, my hands thrust in my pockets, my features carefully blank.

"Keeley. Lovely night for it."

"I'm sorry," she gasps, still rigid with horror. "My cabin doesn't have a hot tub, so I thought... I thought maybe..."

It is extremely clear what she thought, but I can't resist teasing her anyway. She's so adorably embarrassed, squirming in the bubbles in her tiny blue bikini, and I have to swallow down a laugh.

Thank you, Brandon. Thanks for waking me up. Thanks for being an insufferable shit.

"What did you think, Keeley?" My voice is low and quiet, but it cuts through the rush of the bubbles. Keeley darts a glance to the side, like she's trying to judge if she can make a run for it.

I lean forward, my hands resting on the rim of the hot tub.

"I'm waiting. Shall I count to ten?"

"I—oh god. Um. I'm so sorry."

"Yes, you said that part already." I can't help it. A smirk tugs my mouth, and she wilts with relief, huffing and splashing me with drops of warm water.

"I thought you were serious! Holy shit. I thought I was a dead girl."

"I would never murder a student," I assure her, as though I didn't just fantasize about drowning Brandon. "There are rules about things like that."

She laughs, the sound hollow. "Pretty sure there are rules about sneaking into people's hot tubs, too."

I cock my head, watching her closely. Out here in the middle of the night, between the stars and the snow, nothing feels real. Maybe that's why I say it.

"So there are. But you came anyway. Do you want to be punished, Keeley?"

Her mouth parts slightly. Her pupils blow wide, her chest heaving with a shaky breath, and I can see a shiver travel down her body from here. Fuck.

This is getting out of hand. I'm flirting, being so damn obvious, and she's practically naked at my cabin. If anyone saw this, if anyone got wind, I'd be fired faster than I could pack up my office. I push away from the hot tub, backing up a step, and watch her from a safe distance.

As if there were such a thing.

"Why are you awake?" Keeley wisely ignores my question. She draws her knees up to her chest. "I figured you'd be an early night kind of guy."

I shrug, far too pleased that she'd thought of me at all.

"Usual stuff. Patrolling for hot tub bandits."

"Really, though."

"Really?" I blow out a breath, peering up at the night sky. The stars are insane out here, far away from the city lights—a million tiny pinpricks, sparkling in indigo space.

Brandon's shitty music woke me. Sort of. And that's a reasonable thing to say.

But I was already tossing and turning. So damn restless, my head pounding and heart squeezing, just knowing she was so near.

That's not a good thing to say.

"Brandon." I jerk my head back toward the student cabins. "His electro-crap woke me up."

"You're a light sleeper," Keeley murmurs, the words hushed, but there's no missing the longing in her tone. It punches me square in the chest, stealing my breath worse than the cold.

I'm tired. That's all. Imagining things.

There's no way a gorgeous girl like Keeley would want a grumpy old bastard like me.

"Yeah," I rasp. And then, because I've got no fucking judgement, I ask: "Are you?"

Keeley snorts and shakes her head, the wet strands of her hair swirling in the water.

"I sleep like the dead." She leans forward, like she's telling me a secret. "Sometimes I fall asleep still in my clothes."

The image of undressing her—not for creepy reasons, but to tuck her in, to make her comfortable—well, that's going to haunt me for years. Pulling a blanket over her shoulders. Brushing her hair off her forehead.

God.

"Better wake up on time tomorrow," I croak. "Or I'll come banging on your door."

"Don't worry." She grins at me, eyes sparkling. "I'm a morning person, professor."

Her calling me that is like a bucket of icy water down my back. It's exactly what I need—a timely reminder that Keeley is my student. If I keep pushing, keep nudging my toe over this line, I'm a monster. No better than Gideon.

"Enjoy the tub." I back up a step. "Don't stay in too long. It's bad for you."

"Yes, coach." She gives a mock salute, and I turn on my heel before I do something I regret. The deck vibrates under my heavy steps, and the door rattles in the frame as I slam it shut.

* * *

I was so damn set on Keeley coming on this trip, but now that we're here, I've got this creeping sense of dread. It curls in my gut, hooking tighter every time she looks at me.

Which is a lot. I know, because I'm looking at her.

Why the hell did I think this was a good idea? Going away with her, into the mountains where nothing feels real? Yeah, there are other students. Ski instructors and schedules. But everything feels freer out here somehow, untethered from the real world, and that's dangerous.

I need to keep myself in check.

Over the next few days, I stay away from Keeley. I don't brush her off—when she bounces over to talk to me, I talk back and ask questions, but I schedule all her sessions with the other instructors. I tell myself it's better—I'm no great skier, and this way she can learn from the best.

Away from me.

Meals are the hardest. We all eat together in the resort canteen—nothing special, but any hot food after a long day on the slopes tastes like heaven. And though I go to a separate table from the students every single time, she follows me, chattering brightly as she puts down her tray.

I don't have the heart to send her away. Not even when some of the other students glance over, whispering. Brandon watches too, his expression pensive, and that's the most dangerous of all.

I still shift over to make room.

More than anything, I want this trip to be good for her. I want it to live up to her daydreams. I was worried on the first day, when I saw how often she hit the deck, but Keeley is supremely unflappable. She doesn't care if she's not a natural skier. She and Oliver laugh about it, whooping as they execute the most basic moves, and I have to hide my smile behind my glove. And when I see her fresh bruises every night when I walk past her in my hot tub—I stuff my hands in my pockets to keep from reaching for her and soothing that ache.

I should stop walking out at night. Staying up on the off-chance that she might come; that I could catch a glimpse.

It's fucked up.

I'm fucked up.

On the last night after dinner, I pull my phone from my pocket, tugging off my glove with my teeth as I scroll through the contacts. I don't let myself second guess as I press it to my ear, squinting against the whistling wind as I trudge back to the cabins.

"Beck?"

Gideon's voice is shocked in my ear. Like he never thought he'd hear from me again.

Neither did I.

But I'd be the worst kind of hypocrite at this point. And besides—I need to know. I need to hear whether it can work out.

"How's it going?"

Gideon huffs a laugh, the sound crackling in my ear.

"Really? That's it, after months? *How's it going?*"

"Don't be a bitch," I say mildly, stepping over the remains of a snowman. "How's it going? With Lucy?"

There's a wary silence. I can't really blame him. But I'm not calling to judge. I really need to know.

"It's good," he says slowly, the suspicion clear in his voice. "Why?"

"Just asking."

"Bullshit," Gideon says hotly. "Why do you want to know? I swear to god, if you make things hard for her at the college—"

"Jesus Christ, Gid," I interrupt. "How evil do you think I am?" There's a loaded pause. I swallow hard. "I should have called sooner."

"Yeah, you should have."

I grit my teeth. There's nothing for it.

"I've been... what's the word? Projecting."

Gideon blows out a slow breath. "Ah."

Yeah. *Ah.* It's not a small confession. Gideon lost his whole career when he chose Lucy. And I'm the star of my department, their headliner, and who's to say these offers to coach elite athletes won't dry up after a scandal?

"Is she worth it?"

"Yes," I say immediately. But then: "It's not the only question, though. What if I ruin things for her? She gets enough shit as it is, being female in the department. If she hooked up with a professor..."

"Yeah." Gideon clicks his tongue. "If you're not sure, not one hundred percent certain... stay away, man."

"Right." I swallow hard. "Right."

It's good advice. The right thing for him to say, and more than he owes me at this point. It still makes my chest ache.

"It was good to hear from you," he says suddenly. "Don't be a stranger, Beckett."

"I won't." I round the corner and my cabin comes into view. "See you, Gid."

I hang up and stride through the snow to the steps. When I climb onto the deck, I swing around the side of the cabin.

The hot tub hums, steam leaking from under the cover. I peel it back, gazing down at the still depths.

She sat here every night this week. Keeley.

I tug my glove off and touch my palm to the water.

10

Chapter Nine

The last few days have been magical. Unreal. Oh, I still suck at skiing, but my lungs are full of crisp mountain air, and I've been so close to him. Professor Hale.

Everywhere I look, he's there too, and he watches me back as much as I watch him. It's like out here, away from the college campus, his restraint has worn thin.

We go back tomorrow morning. And I know, as sure as I know my own name, that once we're there, a door will slam closed between us. It's barely open a crack as it is, but once all the constant reminders of my student status are everywhere again...

I don't think he'll watch me anymore.

That's why I do it.

I give myself a pep talk. Take a hot shower in the evening and prowl up and down in my tiny chalet, muttering to myself. Good things come to those who are brave. And I am brave.

So there's nothing else for it.

I'm going to snag myself a hot professor.

I wait until it's gone midnight. Until the others are—well,

if not asleep, then wrapped up in their own worlds, at least. Then I bundle myself up in my Llewellyn College sweatshirt and rented ski jacket, and creep out the door.

The cold here is insane. It's a physical blow—a smack to the face every time you step outside. I bite my lip, teeth chattering, as I lock up my cabin and tiptoe down the front steps. The snow crunches under my boots—it's impossible to really creep anywhere in snow—and I wince and check the windows of the nearest cabins.

Nothing. Drawn curtains and the occasional glow of lamplight.

No prying eyes.

Professor Hale's cabin is set away from the students'. If anyone were to look closely, they'd see a trail of footprints leading from my cabin to his deck, to my nightly stolen hot tub session.

Hopefully no one has looked closely. I didn't even think of that.

But then again, I can't bring myself to care, either. Professor Hale wouldn't really get in trouble—I'd just say that I went over to ask questions for class, and the thought of the other students suspecting something doesn't bother me. How could a girl be anything but proud to be linked to Beckett Hale?

The professor's curtains are drawn too, but soft, warm light glows around the edges of the windows.

Good. He'd be grumpy if I woke him up, and I need him to listen to me. To give this a chance. My knock is muffled by my thick glove, but the floorboards creak inside. I hear a muttered curse, and stifle a smile.

"What is it—"

He opens the door, already annoyed to be disturbed, but his

face changes when he sees it's me. His eyebrows twitch up his forehead, but then he locks it all down. Back to unreadable stone.

"What is it, Keeley?" He glances over my shoulder at my cabin. "Are you locked out or something?"

"No." He waits for me to say something else, to explain why I'm here, but my rehearsed speech has flown out of my brain. "Um. Can I come inside?"

Professor Hale blows out a breath. "I don't think that's a good idea. Whatever it is, you'll have to tell me out here."

"Okay," I murmur, miserable. God, what was I thinking, coming here? My eyes fall closed—I can't bear to see his face while I say this. While I admit everything I'm feeling. After all, he freaked out about that one hug, how mad will he be—

A gentle hand takes mine and pulls me into the cabin. The door shuts with a snap.

It's warm. Lit with a golden glow and the crackling warmth of the log burner. Professor Hale's duffel bag is on the bed, the mattress strewn with bits of clothing.

"I was packing," he grunts, scrubbing the back of his head.

"So messy," I murmur, darting him a quick smile. "Like your office."

"It's not that bad."

"It's messy, professor."

He sucks in a deep breath, taking his usual big step back from me.

"What can I do for you, Keeley?"

That's the question, isn't it? The million dollar question. And I'm not ready for the answer yet, so I stall.

"Um. You can sit down."

His mouth twitches. "You came here to make me sit down?"

64

I roll my eyes. "Just do it."

He glances at the bed, and my heart slams in my chest, but he turns on his heel and marches to the plain wooden chair by the wall. He lowers his bulk into it, the chair creaking under his weight. God, he's so solid.

Focus, Keeley.

"Is this another experiment?" he asks mildly. Professor Hale has a reputation for being gruff, even irritable, but he's always so patient with me.

"Something like that." I cross to him, tugging off my gloves and dropping them on the floor. He watches them fall with wary eyes.

"What are you exploring?"

I nudge my way to stand between his legs. Then gather my courage and rest my palms on his shoulders.

"How my professor feels about me," I whisper.

"Keeley." God, he looks tortured. Regret and excitement churn in my stomach. "You already know."

* * *

He's going to send me away. The tension is building in his rigid shoulders; his shadowed eyes keep darting toward the door. This is it, my one big chance to show him I feel the same way.

I take his heavy wrist and place his hand on my waist beneath my ski jacket.

"Keeley."

His fingers scrunch up my sweatshirt; his hand molds tighter to my skin. He's mapping me, squeezing me, and it's perfect. I hum and tip back my head, fishing around for his other hand, then place it on the side of my neck.

His hands are huge. He dwarfs me, cradling the side of my jaw, running his thumb along my pulse point. Can he feel it—the way my heart is racing for him?

"Professor Hale—"

"Beckett." He gusts out a bitter sigh. "If we're doing this, call me Beckett."

I fix him with a look. "Do you want me to leave, Beckett?"

"No." He presses his face into my shoulder. "God help me. No."

"Then try to sound a bit happier, please."

He snorts a laugh, my hair fluttering.

"Oh, I'm happy, Keeley. Wretchedly happy."

As if to prove it, Professor Hale—Beckett—lunges forward and grabs me under the ass. He lifts me into his lap, settling me on his muscled thighs, and the chair screams beneath our joined weight.

"Nope," Beckett says, pushing to stand as I melt into giggles. He lifts me easily, like I'm a featherweight, and not a tall girl with thick muscles and big bones. I wind my arms around his neck—not really to help, but to squirm closer. His beard tickles my cheek.

The floorboards creak as he walks us across the room. I nip at his earlobe, and a thought occurs to me.

"I've never done this before," I whisper, confessing in his ear. I figure he should probably know. He might need to do some extra sexual wizardry. But Beckett stills, the cabin suddenly quiet.

He turns a little, spinning us toward the door, and I have a horrible image of him dumping me out onto his snowy deck. I wriggle closer, locking my ankles behind his back like a monkey.

"Please don't."

He shakes his head. "God, Keeley. If I weren't a bastard before..."

"Please. It doesn't have to be a big deal, does it?"

"If you've been saving yourself—"

I scoff. "I haven't been saving myself. No one's wanted me, and I haven't wanted them." I tug on the back of his sweater, thumping him on the shoulder. "I want *you*. I've wanted you for years. Please." I lean back in his arms, forcing a sly smile. "Do you want me to beg, professor?"

His eyes darken, but not with arousal.

"No," he clips out. "A girl like you shouldn't have to beg for anything, Keeley."

"Well, then." I bounce in his arms, suddenly cheerful. All it takes is a few sweet words from him. He rolls his eyes but turns us back toward the bed, closing the distance in three strides.

I twist in his hold. We both look down at the clothes strewn over the covers.

"I guess it is kind of messy."

"Yeah, but now I get to do this." I hop down to the floor and sweep everything onto the floorboards in one dramatic motion. "It would be more fun with your desk, but you get the idea—"

Two big hands pick me up by the waist and toss me onto the mattress.

"You're going to ruin me, Keeley. Do you hear me?" He crawls up the bed after me, his big body hovering over mine. "You're going to fucking ruin me."

Is that a good thing? The way he says it, grinding it out between his teeth, I can't tell if it's a compliment or a warning. Maybe both.

"Don't worry. I won't tell."

"I didn't mean—" he cuts himself off with a huff. Then dips

his head and seals his mouth to mine.

It's my first kiss. Didn't mention that part, since he got his panties in such a knot over the virgin thing. Still, as first kisses go, it's one for the record books. Professor Hale—Beckett, damn it—is gentle, warm, coaxing me to kiss him back with his signature patience. I do my best, throwing if not any skill then every last scrap of my enthusiasm at the task.

He seems to approve. He groans, the sound vibrating through his chest to mine, dropping lower to press his body against me. I slide my legs open and he slots against me there too, and I can *feel* him. The hard length of his cock.

Sweet Jesus. He's huge everywhere.

I may not make it out alive.

Beckett swipes his tongue along the seam of my lips, and I moan and arch against him. My lips part, then his tongue pushes into my mouth, sweeping to tangle with my own.

I see stars.

"Shit," I gasp when he wrenches his mouth away, kissing a hot trail down my throat.

"Language," he murmurs against my skin. "Keeley, I'm shocked."

"Shut up." I bat his impossibly large shoulder. God, his skeleton is like scaffolding.

"What do you want from me, sweetheart?"

A warm, gooey glow spreads through my veins. I want him to call me sweetheart from now on, for a start.

"Um." This is the problem with being a virgin. Sure, I've seen porn, and I've heard Raine and Lucy talk about stuff like this. But how am I supposed to know what I like until I've tried it? And believe me: I want to try it *all* with Beckett Hale. "What's on the menu?"

He snorts again, drifting down my body to rub his face over my sternum. He makes no move to undress me, to get his hands on bare skin, and I don't know whether that's sweet of him or irritating.

"Whatever you like."

"That's so unhelpful."

"Is it?"

"Yes. Help a virgin out, Prof—Beckett."

"Alright." He pushes up on his hands, high enough to meet my eye. His cheeks are flushed above his beard, and his pupils are blown wide. God, I feel amazing. Powerful. "Shall I tell you what I'd like to do? Then you can decide, yes or no."

"That would be helpful."

"I want to lick you." He smirks as I suck in a shaky breath, then dips down to drag his nose up my hairline. "I want to lick your sweet pussy until you cry."

"Good," I rasp, throat tight. "Yeah. That sounds good."

* * *

"Tell me to stop any time."

"Okay."

"If you change your mind—"

"Beckett."

He pauses, fingers hooked in the waistband of my leggings, and fixes me with a look.

"Humor me, Keeley."

I roll my eyes and hold up the scouts' salute. "I solemnly swear to stop you if I change my mind. But Beckett—" It's my turn to glare. "I'm not going to. Stop trying to talk me out of this."

A sigh shudders out of him, and his head drops. Then my leggings peel down my legs in one smooth motion. I prop myself up on my elbows to watch as Beckett settles between my thighs, his eyes fixed on the green triangle of my panties.

He rubs the pad of one finger over the center of the cotton. I buck off the mattress, blood thrumming in my ears. My sweatshirt slides around my shoulders, the collar frayed and sagging, and I bite my lip and ask the question that's bugging me.

"Are you leaving my clothes on so you don't have to see all of me?"

"No," he clips out. "I don't want you to get cold. And I've seen all of you, remember? In my hot tub."

"Not every inch."

"Enough. Enough to know you're fucking gorgeous. Don't talk about yourself like this, sweetheart."

Yeah, that'll do it. I settle back against the mattress, heart singing, and reach down to idly scratch through his hair. It's softer than I expected.

"What happens ne—"

Wet heat seals over my core, lathing me through my panties, and I yelp, my legs kicking. Beckett hums and presses me down by the hips, running his palms along to press my thighs wide. He licks me steadily, with purpose, and already my muscles shake.

"Do you always leave the panties on?"

"Keeley." The hum of my name spreads to my clit. "Are you going to ask questions all the way through?"

"Maybe." I tug on his hair. "I'm here to learn, professor."

His groan makes my toes curl. He mutters something to himself, but it sounds like *definitely going to hell.*

The tip of his finger hooks my panties to the side, and this time when he licks me, I feel it *all*. It's hot and wet and smooth, the rasp of his beard tickling my thighs, and I scrunch the bed covers up in both fists to keep from grabbing his head and rubbing all over him.

A broad finger strokes at my entrance.

"Shit," I hiss. It dips inside, just to the first knuckle, but it's big. So much bigger than my own fingers.

"You like it?"

"Uh-huh." I squirm, trying to nudge him deeper. "Beckett, if that's the size of your *finger*—"

"Stop it, sweetheart. My ego will explode."

He laps at my clit as his finger pumps in and out, pushing further and further each time. When he crooks it up, rubbing against a spot on my inner walls, I let out a yelp and clap a hand over my mouth.

I can't scream and yell out like we're in our own porno. There are students nearby.

But god, I want to. And if it wouldn't hurt Beckett, wouldn't land him in trouble, I'd freaking love for everyone to know that I'm his. That he wants me, and I want him, and we're doing this together.

Every lap of his tongue, every scrape of his teeth and every moan that vibrates through my core, it all winds me tighter and tighter. I'm spring-loaded, coiling up until my muscles shake and I can't breathe, tugging desperately at Beckett's hair.

He slides another finger inside me, crooking them both, and I shatter. I fall apart with a hoarse cry, my hips bucking, his tongue lathing me through it, every point of my focus narrowed in to where he's touching me. Licking me.

"God." When every last wave of sensation has pulsed through

me, I collapse into a trembling heap. Is it normal for the backs of my knees to be sweaty? "That was... god."

He crawls up beside me, brushing my hair off my forehead. It's so tender, I could cry.

"A good first time?"

"The best."

His mouth quirks, and I reach up to scratch at his beard. He hums and pushes into my hand like a cat, and it's so domestic.

I could do this everyday. Every damn day for the rest of my life.

A knock at the door freezes us both. My heart slams into my throat, and I nod jerkily when Beckett presses a finger against his lips.

He fixes himself quickly, adjusting his pants and scrubbing his sleeve over his face. I badly want to pull my leggings up my bare legs, but I don't want to make a sound, so I tuck my knees inside my baggy sweatshirt.

Cold mountain air swirls in as Beckett cracks open the door. There are low murmurs; a nod from Beckett. Then boots thud against his decking as the person walks away, and Beckett closes the door with a snap.

"Who was it?"

Beckett waves off my question, eyes distant.

"It doesn't matter. Time to go, sweetheart. You need some sleep."

It's a dismissal, and we both know it is, but I tamp the hurt down. He's already risked so much for me tonight. And it's not like I can sleep over in the teacher's cabin. After a pause, Beckett crosses to the bed and helps me pull my leggings back up, then tucks my hair behind my ear.

It's okay. The rising hurt and panic subside.

"Go straight back to your cabin." His kiss is gentle on my forehead. "I'll watch from the window to make sure you get back safe."

How could this man ever think he was bad for me? He's like a warm bath. A hot chocolate with marshmallows on a freezing cold day.

"Goodnight, Beckett."

"Goodnight, sweetheart."

I carry that nickname in my chest, all the way back across the snow.

Chapter Ten

A deafening silence falls once she's gone. I cross to the window, heart in my throat, and watch Keeley trudge back through the snow. Joy and shame war inside me, and I don't know whether to punch the air or bash my head against the wall.

God.

What have I done?

Her closeness, the sight and scent of her, her hands on me—it addled my brains. Clouded my judgement. And now I've put her in the worst possible position: a subject of gossip, of speculation. If anyone suspects what happened here tonight... all her hard-earned progress is at risk.

I don't think he saw her. When I cracked the door open and saw Brandon there, my blood froze in my veins. Not for me—god knows it's too late for that—but for her. I didn't want Keeley's first time to be marred. To become the butt of a joke.

But Brandon asked some dull question about the assignment due next week. Said he was up late studying, had a question, and saw the lights on in my cabin. Surely a little shit like him would have crowed with victory if he caught a glimpse of Keeley on my bed. It would be Christmas come early for that jackass—the chance to humiliate the girl who consistently beats him, and the coach who benched him from the team.

No. No, he can't have seen her.

It doesn't change things for me, of course. There's no way I can go back to the college, can walk through the department corridors and hold court in lecture theaters after what I've done.

I can't teach anymore. It's as simple as that.

I still can't bring myself to regret it.

The clock on my phone shows 2:13am. I chew on the inside of my cheek, considering, then mutter a curse and dial. Fraser will have bigger worries than lost beauty sleep when he hears what I've done. He answers on the fifth ring, voice gravelly from sleep, irritation thick in his tone.

"What, Beckett? I swear to god, if you're not seriously injured you soon will be."

"Not very patient," I say mildly. Apparently even now, I can't help myself. "I hope you're nicer to the students."

"The students don't call me at 2am."

I take a deep breath. "They might if they fuck up badly enough."

There's a loaded silence. A distant rustling and the creak of a headboard. Then: "Explain."

I wince, scrubbing the back of my head. Yeah, I've set myself up nicely here. I was so damn judgemental of Gideon that there's no room for sympathy for me.

Boo hoo. Poor deviant professor. I roll my eyes, sick to the back teeth with my own bullshit.

"I slept with her," I say shortly.

"Who?" Fraser barks.

Oh yeah. I never told him about Keeley. Here I've been, going through my days, weeks and months, carrying the thought of her in my heart like something precious, and I neglected to ever mention that to my friends.

Because I knew what it would sound like. A perverted old man; a creep.

My gut churns queasily. Does Keeley think that? Will she now, once the endorphins fade?

"My student. Keeley."

Fraser's string of curses would make a mobster weep. I blink, half surprised, half impressed, but then his rant turns to full sentences.

"What the fuck is going on? Is there something in the water? Both of you, sleeping with students?"

"I'm sorry, man."

"Don't you fucking lie to me!"

It's terrible of me, truly a dick move on my part, but I can't hide a strangled laugh. I've never heard Fraser lose his shit like this. When Gideon confessed to what happened with Lucy, I guess some part of him must have expected it. We knew they had history, after all, and he always looked so wistful when he mentioned her.

I've given no warning. No heads up. I haven't confided in Fraser, sought his better judgement—maybe because I knew what he'd say.

He'd have told me to keep away. To transfer the course to another professor, and stay as far away from Keeley as I could get.

Not possible. That's why I'm in this mess.

"Alright. I'm not sorry. But it's done now, and I need to know the next steps."

"The next steps?" Fraser splutters. "Are you kidding me? Are you not the same Beckett who frog-marched Gideon to his office, who escorted him off campus then never spoke to him again?"

"I called him, actually. Earlier. To ask his advice."

"And he told you to do this?" Fraser sounds incredulous. Like he can't believe he has such a pair of dip-shits for friends. All his earlier sleepiness is gone, and he bites each word down the phone like he wants to wring my neck.

It's a fair reaction.

"No. Gid told me to stay away."

"Well, he was right."

I grind my teeth. I shouldn't be hurt by this. I shouldn't be petulant, all because Gideon got the understanding Fraser and I've got the sleep-deprived lectures.

But I thought he knew me better. Knew that I'd never do this out of mere attraction, that I'd only risk everything for someone I truly loved.

And god, I have loved Keeley. Even now, having one of the worst conversations of my life, bliss bubbles up inside my chest at the thought of her.

I tamp it down. I've had my moment of weakness—now it's time to do what's right. To protect her, to keep her safe from rumors and repercussions, and to walk away. To let her find someone her own age. Someone who won't bring her disgrace.

"You still there?" Fraser asks carefully, like he's regretting the force of his rant. I shake myself, eyes burning, and clear my throat before I speak.

"Yeah, man. I'm still here."

He's a good friend, really. He lays out the next steps with

patience, even as his voice is tight with anger, and he warms slightly when he realizes that I'm going to do this properly. I'm not going to try to keep my job or even stay in the area.

That coaching job called earlier. They want me on the coast by the end of next week.

12

Chapter Eleven

I wake up like a fairy tale princess cliche. Birds chirping; sun shining. When I sit up in bed and stretch, my shoulders pop in a really delicious way.

Wow. Last night was...

Everything.

I pack in a blur, throwing tangled up leggings and ski goggles at my backpack, then run in and out of the tiny bathroom three times before I remember my toothbrush. I've always been a bit scattered, but this is something else.

This is Beckett. He's overloaded my senses. Distracted me with his soft, raspy beard and his clean manly scent and the careful way he touched me. Like I was fragile. Delicate. Precious.

As I wrestle my overstuffed backpack closed, there's only one question on my mind: when can we do that again?

Because he must want to, right? He doesn't seem like the kind of man who risks his career over a simple fling. And the way he held me, the things he whispered to me—Beckett Hale has wanted this as long as I have. Longer, maybe.

A voice prods at the back of my brain, pointing out all the things that could go wrong. The barriers, the risks, the potential cost. I brush it away, because it's Beckett, and I've never been so sure about anything.

I don't care about all the reasons not to do this. I've never been a coward, and I won't start now.

Besides, that bridge has burned to a crisp. It caught alight the minute I stepped into his cabin after midnight. Hell—the minute I sneaked into his hot tub and he looked at me with hungry eyes.

The cabin door squeaks on its hinges as I drag it shut behind me. I spin the key in the lock, squinting against the blinding sunshine bouncing off the snow. It's early, just gone dawn, and all around are the shouts and crunching footsteps of the students emptying out of the cabins. The mountain looms behind us, all rocky peaks and perfect white drifts, and I take a moment to say a silent goodbye.

I suck at skiing.

Still the best few days of my life.

Maybe one day we'll come back. Beckett and I. Maybe we could rent a little cabin with a hot tub, like a normal couple, and he could teach me more about skiing on the slopes. Or he could go off and enjoy himself, off on the hard routes, and we could meet up for hot chocolates afterwards. Maybe—

I shake my head, trudging through the snow toward the bus idling a hundred feet away. Steam pours out of its exhaust, billowing up in a misty column, and the windows are fogged over from the cold. I can see my breath as I walk over, my backpack hitched high on my shoulder.

"Good night?"

Brandon's voice makes me jump. I shoot him a wary smile,

rubbing a hand over my sweater-clad chest.

"Yeah, yeah it was good. Um. Pretty quiet. Just went to sleep early. You?"

We don't do this. Brandon doesn't make small talk with me; since our failed group project, he barely even looks at me. As though *I'm* the one who wrecked his grade. Ass.

Still, I'm compulsively polite—it's one of Raine's greatest frustrations with me—so I play along and chat. Like we're fine. Like we're friends.

"Oh, yeah." Brandon grins at me, his teeth as sparkling white as the snow. "Yeah, I took a walk. The stars are amazing out here after midnight."

Unease tickles at the back of my neck. That knock on Beckett's door...

"I bet." I swallow, darting him another look. Brandon smiles at me, face pleasant. "So, uh. Did you like the trip?"

He waves a gloved hand, brushing the question away.

"Obviously. No, Keeley, the question is: did *you* have a good time?" His mouth twitches like he's amusing himself. "Was it everything you dreamed?"

Okay, this is officially weird. I huff and speed up, marching toward the bus. Brandon keeps stride with me easily, but he can't force me to talk. I tune him out, like an irritating bug. He prods and wheedles, trying to get a reaction, but I don't give him one. Does he think he's the first jackass I've ever had to deal with? The trick is to ignore them, outlast them, and they'll eventually get bored. Sure enough, he yells at one of the other guys and jogs off as we reach the back of the bus.

"Everything alright?"

Beckett stands six feet away, a frown creasing his forehead. His eyes follow Brandon's back, the hood of his designer ski jacket bouncing as he jogs through the snow.

God. Beckett. Professor Hale. Is it still a crush after you've hooked up with a person? Because it sure feels like a crush. I'm still blushing, still squirming from excitement and nerves. I'd trade my left pinkie finger to be able to run at him and jump into those burly arms.

"I'm good." I beam at him, trudging closer. "I'm perfect, professor."

He flinches at the title.

… Okay.

I look at him again, more closely this time. His nose is pink from the cold, his puffy ski jacket exaggerating the breadth of his shoulders. His eyes are shadowed and tired, and a muscle tics in his temple as he clenches his jaw.

I cast a glance around, then lean in. "Are *you* okay?"

He nods and steps back, his movements curt. My heart sinks all the way down to my snow boots, my fingers growing numb where they grip my bag strap.

No. He's not… he's not doing this. Not pretending nothing happened. He's being careful, that's all, while there are students around. I force myself to nod and smile, moving past him to the bus steps.

* * *

I sit in the same row as I did on the way here: the second row back from the front. The one behind Beckett. I wait for what feels like an eternity, twisting the frayed cuffs of my sleeves, and when he finally climbs the steps into the bus, I hold my breath.

Beckett lowers himself into the seat in front of me. He doesn't even glance in my direction.

Okay.

Okay.

This is fine. He's being careful, protecting our reputations. I can—I understand that. I gnaw on my bottom lip, staring at the back of his head as he leans forward, the bus lurching away from the sidewalk, the wheels groaning over the snow. I want to talk to him so badly. Want to see his kind, patient gaze; want to feel his big hand wrap around mine and squeeze.

I blow out a breath, settling back in my seat. It's a long drive, and I'm acting crazy.

Snow-capped mountains slide past as we drive away, and I watch the scenery with drooping eyelashes. As the adrenaline of this morning fades, leaving only a dull ache in my chest, my head starts to droop, bouncing off the bus window. I blink, bleary-eyed and catch Beckett staring at me in the reflection.

I suck in a breath.

He looks away.

My scarf is kind of musty as I pull it up over my nose, but I don't care. I want to burrow deep into these layers and never come out. The warmth of the wool, my own minty breath washing over my cheeks, the gentle rocking of the bus...

I fall into a troubled sleep.

One with hazel eyes staring at me, then turning away.

One where Brandon's laughter echoes through my brain.

I wake to a gentle hand on my shoulder. Beckett squeezes gently, frowning over me until I blink awake, then he snatches his hand back and crosses his arms.

"We're here, Keeley. You slept the whole way."

No *sweetheart* today, then.

But I guess he wasn't ignoring me completely. I huff and

unclip my seat belt, sliding out of the row. The bus is empty except for a few other stragglers, pulling their bags out of the luggage racks with pale, drawn faces. Beckett leans over, shaking someone else awake, and my eyes drop automatically to his ass.

"Look alive, Keeley." Brandon winks at me from the bus doorway. His smile is sly, like he knows exactly where I was looking.

Whatever. As if I'm the first student to ogle a teacher.

It's evening on campus, the sky tinted pink about the rooftops. Lights are switching on, lighting up classrooms and office like fishbowls, and the last few industrious students stroll between the library and the campus coffee shop. White and gray pigeons scrap and flutter by the benches, fighting over dropped crumbs.

I hitch my backpack up on my aching shoulders and debate waiting.

Will he even talk to me?

It's a sour thought, and one that I'd never thought I'd have about Beckett Hale. Even if he regretted what he did, even if he didn't want to do it again, I'd never have expected him to brush me off quite so coldly. This morning, I could tell myself it was because we had an audience. That he was been cautious—protective, even.

But there was no one watching when he held my gaze in the reflection. When he watched me, face blank, then turned away.

My snow boots thud against the paving stones as I cross to the nearest bench, dropping my backpack on the floor and scattering the pigeons. I collapse onto the slotted wood, tired down to my bone marrow.

I have to talk to him. Try and understand, at least. Then I can go home, take a scalding hot shower, and cry. My throat is dry from not drinking all day, and my stomach is cramping from hunger.

I'll go and look after myself. Like I always have.

The bus empties quickly, everyone keen to drag their aching asses home to do laundry and catch up on sleep. Everyone except Brandon, apparently. He waltzes over and sits next to me, his thigh brushing against mine.

I roll my eyes and slide away. Man-spreaders. Honestly.

"I don't think he wants to talk, Keeley."

Brandon says it in a stage whisper, like he's confiding in me. I stiffen, back straight.

"I have a question about class."

"Sure you do."

Okay. I've had about enough of Brandon as I can stomach. He's bad enough when I'm well-fed.

"Spit it out." I turn to him, mouth pressed in a tight line. "Whatever you have to say, get it over with."

Brandon's not bothered by my tone. He leans back, relaxed, laying his arm along the back of the bench behind me. I jerk forward when his fingers play in my hair.

"Don't touch me."

"Why?" Brandon's grin is savage. "Because I can't give you good grades?"

"Because I will smear you over the sidewalk, you piece of shit."

Something flickers behind his eyes, something violent and bitter, but he pulls his arm back. Maybe he's remembering all those times I kicked his ass in the gym.

It's not an empty threat. I think I'm a nice person overall, but if he touches me again, I'll break his freaking nose. And maybe he can read that in my face, because he drops his stupid friendly pretense and leans in.

"I know you're fucking him, Keeley. And that explains so much. No wonder you've been top of the class."

"I beat you because I'm better than you."

He draws in a sharp breath through his nose. "Bullshit. You're fucking him and he's grading you higher."

"Oh yeah?" I lean in close to match him, our noses inches away. "Explain how I beat you in the practicals, then. Can't fake that, asshole."

He opens his mouth and closes it, cheeks flushing an ugly red, and I'm done with this loser. I push to my feet, frown fixed on the bus where Beckett watches us, his arms crossed and feet planted.

Yeah, he's not coming over here. And suddenly, I'm done with these chicken shit men. I may not be the next top model or whatever, but I am smart and hardworking and a freaking catch. I don't need to cheat my way into the top grades, and I don't need to chase after men who ignore me.

But goddamn, I need Raine's chocolate chip cookie dough like I need my next breath.

"I'm out." I scoop my backpack up, kicking Brandon's foot out the way with extra force. "Spread whatever rumors you want. You won't be the first mediocre man to do it and you won't be the last. But just know, every time I humiliate you in class, your weak-ass grumbling brings me joy. And one day, when you're shit at your job and you hate your wife and you've wasted every privilege you were born with out of sheer stupidity, I will think of your misery and I will smile."

Then, because apparently I can't help myself, I turn to Beckett and flip him off before walking away.

I don't need a cab. My rage will carry me home faster than

any set of wheels in the evening rush hour.

And besides, I don't want to explain my damp eyes and flushed, angry cheeks to a stranger.

Chapter Twelve

Something is off.

That rich little weasel is saying something to Keeley. Something *impolite.*

I'll grind him under my heel if he's not careful.

I wait, impatience and anger building in my gut as the last few students stagger from the bus, their movements excruciatingly slow.

"Come on," I clip out, not bothering to turn around. They mumble, but shuffle along faster.

What is he saying? When Brandon came to my cabin last night, I thought for sure we were screwed. But he didn't mention Keeley, didn't gloat at all, and since when did he have any amount of impulse control? He just asked about the assignment then strolled off into the night.

My gut churns as I watch them, Keeley tense and straight-backed on the bench. Whatever he's saying to her, it isn't good, and the timing is too suspicious. He must have suspected, must have seen her tracks—maybe he went and knocked on her cabin door. I chew on the inside of my cheek, watching them, trying to untangle the snarl of my angry thoughts and figure out what to do.

If I go over there, I'll confirm everything he's saying. I'll make things so much worse for her. So I stand my ground, watching and straining to hear, but they're too far away.

Leave, I will Brandon. Get the fuck out of here.

I need to check on her, never mind that I swore I'd leave her alone. I just need to make sure she's okay. But Keeley pushes to her feet, snatching up her backpack, and when she turns to me, fury sparks in her eyes.

She flips me off—the sweetest girl I know, who barely uses curse words—and stomps away, her shoulders tense.

My strides eat up the ground before Brandon can even react. He jerks back against the bench, eyes wide as he stares up at me.

"What did you say to her?"

Cold calculation slides through his expression. He's remembered he has the upper hand—or at least, he thinks he does.

"Why?" God, this kid is ugly when he lets his real self shine through. His normally handsome features contort, and his skin goes all blotchy. "What's it to you, professor?"

He hisses the last word, triumph blazing through his eyes, and I've had about as much of him as I can stomach.

"Good news, Brandon." I grab a fistful of his sweater, yanking him to his feet with my knuckles pressed against this throat. He dangles in my grip—this asshole has probably never fought a day in his life. Goddamn it, it wouldn't even be a fair match, and that's bizarrely disappointing. "I'm not your professor anymore."

He slaps at my hand, struggling to find his feet.

"You can't kick me out of college. You're the one fucking a

89

student—"

"Nope. I quit last night. So what I have or haven't done with Keeley is irrelevant." I draw him closer, letting the full force of my loathing fill my eyes. "There's more good news, Brandon." I shake him, hard. "I can do whatever I want with *you*, too. No one likes a gossip, jackass."

Fear and alarm creep into his blue eyes, and it's that more than anything that pulls me back to myself. I throw him down with a disgusted huff, his limbs sprawling in his designer ski kit.

"Get the fuck out of here."

I don't have to say it twice. I scrub a hand over my beard, watching him sprint away, his ski jacket billowing behind him.

He forgot his backpack. Oh, well.

I scoop it up and toss it into the bushes. Anger and heat are still coursing through my body, and I throw it harder than I meant to, half flattening a shrub.

Shit. Well, I'm not painting myself in glory today. Fraser will freak when he hears I threatened a student.

I don't regret it. The way Keeley stiffened as he spoke, the color draining from her face...

Fuck. What did he say to her?

The only way to know is to ask her, and judging from the look she threw me before she left, she doesn't want to speak to me. It's fair—I've been pushing her away all day, when if everything was right with the world, I'd be gathering her into my arms. Telling her she's beautiful. Kissing her forehead; treating her like the prize she is.

The whole point of not doing those things was to protect her reputation. But if Brandon knows, if he even suspects...

It's too late.

I pushed her away for nothing.

"Jesus, Mary and Joseph." I shake my head, turning back to the bus to scoop up my abandoned duffel.

I've caused nothing but pain for this girl. The sooner I leave for the coast, the better.

* * *

I get the call two beers in, propping up the bar in an old Irish pub a few blocks from my apartment. I'm not drunk—it takes more than a couple of beers to fell a big bastard like me. Try more like a wheelbarrow. But I still mumble as I answer my phone, not in the mood to chat to anyone.

"'Lo?"

"Beck?" I straighten when I hear Gideon's voice. Of course—he's the one I should commiserate with. He might not know what it's like to lose the girl, but he knows the dangerous waters of falling in love with a student.

Even if he pulled it off far better than me. Damn, I don't want to resent him again.

"What's up?" I frown and swig from my beer as he speaks. Then slam the bottle down, nearly spitting over the bar at his next words.

"Uh. I'm with Keeley."

"What? Why?" I growl. Since when am I a territorial asshole? Since now, apparently.

Gideon huffs, the noise crackling down the phone.

"Because she lives with my girlfriend, jackass. Damn it Beckett, you're making it really hard to like you right now."

"It's a fair question—"

"No, not that. I'm talking about Keeley walking in here and

91

bursting into tears." He lowers his voice, like he's worried someone might overhear him. "Seriously, man? You slept with her then finished with her? She says you didn't even have the guts to tell her."

Yeah, that sounds bad. I am definitely the monster in this tale.

"Didn't you do basically the same thing?"

He splutters, then goes quiet.

"Okay," he says eventually, "whatever it is, just—fix it, alright? If you don't want her, tell her. Suck it up. She deserves a conversation. Keeley's a sweet girl."

I know that. God, does he think I don't know that? I've only been in love with her for years. Keeley's *my* fucking sweet girl, but somehow having a meltdown over that seems a poor move. I bite my tongue, swallowing back the words with effort.

He's right. Gideon's right.

I've been so twisted up with trying to protect her, I haven't even told her what's going on. She probably thinks I had one taste of her then changed my mind.

I grip the edge of the bar, suddenly ill.

"Where is she?"

"I'm not giving out her address."

"Gideon, I swear to God. Where is she?"

"I'm serious—"

"I'm not going to blow the fucking door down. I'm going to do what you said. I'm gonna talk to her. And then if she wants me to leave, I'll go."

I wait, breath stalled in my chest as he mulls it over. Then: "I'll ask Lucy. She can text you the address if she thinks it's okay."

"Oh, you little—"

Gideon hangs up, and the bartender eyes me as I curse loudly, snatching up my beer. I take a long pull, then jerk as my phone buzzes on the bar.

Gideon: This is Lucy. You'd better not come here to mess her around.

Then her address, spelled out on my screen.
I slap a bill down on the bar and run for the door.

14

Chapter Thirteen

Raine collapses on the rug, her dark ponytail in disarray. Lucy's sprawled next to the sofa, chest heaving in her sports bra, her head pillowed on Gideon's thigh as he sits on the sofa and reads. Now and then, his eyes flick away from the manuscript in his hand and down to Lucy's shining chest. His gaze darkens, then he catches my raised eyebrow and shrugs.

Apparently Gideon doesn't feel the same need to make me feel better as the girls. He flatly refused to join in my insane workout video.

"I'm not dressed appropriately," he said, palms held up in surrender, but I saw him wink at Lucy.

Usually, I'd find their obvious infatuation sweet, but today it makes bitterness clench in my stomach. This is what Beckett and I should have been. Professor and student turned lovers, our relationship uncomplicated and pure.

So, since I'm petty today, I pick the hardest video in the series and work the three of us into sweaty puddles on the rug.

"Enough." Raine raises a weak hand, face pressed into the

floor. "I don't like anyone this much, Keeley."

"Agreed," Lucy groans. "When I was sad about Gideon, we drank vodka and watched movies. Let's do *that*."

Gideon's fingers slide through Lucy's hair, his mouth twisting at the mention of her being sad.

So.

Not.

Fair.

I flop back on the rug and scowl at the ceiling, strands of purple hair sticking to my forehead. This was supposed to make me feel better—was supposed to sweat all the anger and heartache from my pores.

Instead, my chest aches and I have a stitch.

Two hard knocks on the front door make me groan and sit up. I may or may not have ordered half the menu from the nearest Thai place in my self pity. It seemed like such a good idea forty minutes ago, but now my stomach lurches at the thought of food.

"Coming," I grumble, pushing my sweaty, ruined body to its feet. I sway on the spot, huffing with exhaustion.

The delivery guy from the Thai place is no stranger to seeing me at my lowest. I've answered the door to him in baggy t-shirts stained with pasta sauce; in my fluffy bath robe; in last year's Halloween costume. So I don't even bother to wipe the strands of hair off my sweaty face before I wrench the door open.

Beckett stands in the hall, arms hanging awkwardly at his sides. His face is tight.

"Keeley," he breathes. "We need to talk."

I burst out laughing. It's not the funny kind of laughter. Not a shared joke or real amusement. I just can't believe what I'm hearing. The universe must have a kooky sense of humor.

Beckett frowns, confused. "Why is that funny?"

I snort, shaking my head and grinning down at my feet.

"It's not." I scrub my face with my bare arm. "It's really not."

"Okay." He raises his palms like he's trying to settle a spooked horse. "That's—okay. Sweetheart, please let me in."

That name makes a traitorous bubble of joy well up in my chest. I clear my throat, ignoring it.

"I'd rather talk out here."

Beckett glances over my shoulder, and behind me forced conversation breaks out. Someone puts the next workout video on, while Raine curses loudly.

"Working out?" His mouth tugs up at one corner. My chest throbs so hard I can barely breathe.

"Beckett," I grind out. "What do you want?"

It's a layered question. And I want to hear it all: what he wants right now, here in my apartment hallway. What he wants from me. Just… what he *wants.*

He shifts his weight from side to side. Every time I see him, I've forgotten how big he really is. Beckett Hale is substantial in the way a cargo ship is substantial. Sleek and perfectly designed, but really freaking huge with it. I'm surprised his shoulders don't catch on the walls.

"I wanted to check you're okay. Earlier—I didn't mean to brush you off. I was trying to protect you, keep you safe from gossip. Then Brandon…"

"Yeah." I choke out another laugh. "Yeah, that's a lost cause."

He looks so wrecked at that. Sorrow and regret cling to his features, and his throat bobs beneath his dark beard.

"I'm so sorry, Keeley."

My heart twists. "I'm not."

96

He keeps talking like he didn't even hear me.

"I'm going to fix this, okay? I've already resigned. I've taken another job on the coast, and maybe there will be rumors for a few weeks, but they'll move on soon. I won't let this ruin your life, sweetheart."

I hum, picking at a loose thread on the waistband of my leggings. "On the coast?"

"Yeah." Beckett shrugs, his eyes wide and pleading. "I'm doing the right thing for you. Walking away."

I cross my arms over my chest. The sweat on my skin is cooling fast, making me shiver in the dark hallway. I stare at the man I wanted for so long—the man I was so freaking happy to finally be with.

"Okay," I rasp at last. "If that's what you want."

"It's not what I want, it's what's best for you."

Lord save me from this man. This gorgeous, patient, kind, clueless, infuriating man. I've never been a violent person, but right now I could cheerfully stab Beckett Hale in the eye. The floorboards creak as I step forward, jabbing a finger at his chest.

"Oh, no. Don't do that. Don't make those shitty excuses." I suck in a deep breath and meet his eyes. Let him see the raw anger coiling through me. "Only *I* know what's best for me. You're just taking my choices away and calling it kindness. Well, it's not kindness."

I step back again, crossing my arms. "It's cowardice."

Beckett blinks at me, shocked into silence by my tirade. I guess I'm not usually a ranter. But I'm sick to the back teeth of all of this—the heartache, the longing, the soaring hopes and the crushing disappointment.

Surely it's not supposed to be this hard?

"Here's what I just heard." My voice is hoarse, my breath

catching, but I force myself to keep going. "You're not a professor anymore and you still don't want to be with me. You still think us together is wrong." I raise my chin and wait.

He shudders out a breath.

"Keeley."

I've heard enough. I shoot him a pointed smile and back up into my apartment.

"Have a good life, Professor Hale. Good luck on the coast."

I shut the door.

* * *

I stare blankly at the painted blue wood. Has that scratch always been there?

"Come on." Raine tugs me by the elbow, leading me back to the sofa. The workout video is still blaring, a row of sweat-slicked women dropping into squats. Lucy has migrated from the floor onto Gideon's lap, but she shuffles onto the cushion beside him when she sees my face.

"Oh, Keeley." She reaches out and grips my broad, callused hand in her tiny one. "I'm so sorry."

I nod, too numb and jumbled up to talk. I crash down next to her, the sofa skidding back an inch.

A minute later, Raine pushes a mug of something hot into my hand. I sniff it, nose wrinkling. It's one of her herbal teas.

"Drink up." She drops down on my other side. "It's good for you."

Every last person on this goddamn earth seems to think they know what's good for me. I scowl at her and roll my eyes, but take a sip, because at least Raine is right.

Gross. Tastes like a hot puddle. I breathe through my mouth

instead, and force down another gulp.

"There will be other men," Lucy says.

"Please stop talking."

"Beckett's an idiot," Gideon puts in.

"That's more like it."

And maybe I would feel better if I ranted about him. If I called him names and cursed him out and pulled apart all his flaws.

I can't do it. Even when he's not here, I want to stand up for him. Protect him from anything bad.

I guess we have that in common. Too bad he goes about it all the wrong way.

"Where's that Thai food?" I grumble, nestling down in the cushions. Raine knocks my knee with hers.

"There's my girl."

It will be fine. It will.

He's just a man. Just my first love. It hurts, but it will get better. I tip my head back against the sofa and sigh.

It will get better.

15

Chapter Fourteen

T*he first letter*

Keeley,

I swore not to come to your address uninvited. But does a piece of paper count? Maybe I'm kidding myself. If so, if you'd rather tear your hair out than read my words, then tear this up for confetti, sweetheart. I promise I won't bother you after this.

I want to set a few things straight. The more I think about where I went wrong with you, the more sickened I feel. How could I let things get so badly out of hand? How could I go so wrong with you—*you*, the girl I was half of out my mind in love with for years?

Because I was, Keeley. I was all yours before you even spared me a second glance.

Every day I saw you on campus, it was like my heart would burst out my goddamn chest. I tried to hide it—I didn't want to make you uncomfortable—but surely you noticed the way my hands shook when I passed you your assignments? Surely you noticed how, when you were in the room, I had eyes for no one else?

Keeley, I might as well have walked around with a massive sign on my forehead. I'm yours, sweetheart. I've always been yours.

Maybe you don't want me anymore, not after I made you feel so rotten and unwanted. How can I blame you? You're quite right, sweetheart, as always. You always make the right call, after all.

There's no one's judgement I trust more than yours. So if you see no hope for us, I'll trust that too.

But Keeley, know that I'm here waiting for you. Thinking of you. Writing sappy letters for you.

Beckett

* * *

The second letter

Keeley,

Okay, I know I said I'd only write the one letter. But now that I've started, I find I can't stop. There are so many things I need to say to you—so many conversations I dreamed about us having, and now the chance is gone.

Do you like rowing?

For some reason, I need to know this more than I need air. It's my job at the moment, I suppose, and it's a good one too, but I want to know what you think.

You'd make a good rower, sweetheart. They're all tall and strong and hardworking, like you.

Beckett

* * *

The fifth letter

Keeley,

Most men might be put off by your radio silence. It's probably (definitely) wishful thinking, but I'm taking your lack of a restraining order to mean 'please go on'.

I've been thinking about it, and I think I'd like us to live in the mountains one day. I could teach you to ski—for real, this time—and we could breathe that pine fresh air. We'd spend our days bundled up in dozens of layers, and our nights peeling them off each other.

Think about it, sweetheart.

I'd make it worth your while.

Beckett

* * *

The first reply (unsent)

Beckett,

I do like rowing.

I got top marks this semester. Everyone keeps whispering about why you left.

Did it ever even cross your mind to stay?

Keeley

16

Chapter Fifteen

I prowl between the lines of rowing machines, the hiss and whir of the motors mingling with pained grunts on all sides. The warehouse roller doors are wide open, briny sea air washing in to cool everyone's flushed faces.

They all want to be out there. Cutting through choppy, steel gray waves and catching glimpses of fins.

But if they want to break records, if they want to be extraordinary, they have to put the work in *here*. On the machines, where it's boring and painful and endless.

Hey. If it were easy, everyone would do it.

"Coach?" someone grits out.

I check my watch. There's no way they're nearly done, but I look to show willing.

"Eight more minutes."

Someone groans through their teeth. Yeah, eight minutes can feel a lot like eight years.

"Visualize it!" I clap my hands together, rubbing them for warmth as I walk up and down. Everyone else may be sweating and flushed, but I'm freezing my ass off in this breezy warehouse. "You're rowing against the tide. There are big swells. Choppy waves. The wind and rain battering down at you as you just. Keep. Pushing."

Their breath catches, and they push harder. Faster.

I nod, pleased, and glance at my watch. Seven more minutes. Do I have seven more speeches?

A throat clears over by the warehouse doorway. A figure huddles by the wall, bundled up in a thick winter coat. Spring is an afterthought on this part of the coast—a week long riot between winter and summer. We're still stuck in frosty mornings and winds that blow straight through to your bones.

"Yes?" I squint at the figure. The sun rising behind them throws them into shadow.

The back of my neck prickles.

"Six more minutes," I tell the athletes, then stride between the machines, my heart thudding in my chest. The figure pushes away from the wall, furry hood pulled sideways by the wind.

A lock of light purple hair streams out.

Keeley.

A hoarse sound leaves my mouth. I might be embarrassed if I could think straight, but all I can do is stagger toward her. She pushes her hood back and steps inside the shelter, her mouth twisting in a rueful smile.

Two months. Almost two months since I've seen her. I swallow hard against the lump in my throat. My brain scrambles for reasons that she might be here, excuses for her being in the area, but I come up blank.

Hope sears through me, hot and bright.

"I got your letters." She holds up a crumpled stack of papers. Damn, I wrote to her a lot. She must think I'm insane.

"You never replied." It's not an accusation. I don't know what it is. I just want her to keep talking.

Keeley peers over my shoulder, then offers me a smirk.

"Still a hard ass, then."

I check my watch, then bellow over my shoulder.

"Four minutes!" A series of desperate groans echoes around the warehouse, but I ignore them all and turn back to her.

To Keeley.

She starts to say something else, something light and flirty and fun, but I can't handle it. I hold up a palm.

"Don't toy with me, sweetheart. Why are you here?"

She fiddles with my letters, rocking her weight from side to side. She actually looks nervous, and how can that be possible? How can she not know that I'd take anything she offered and be grateful?

"I miss you," she says at last. "I know it's been a while, but, um. Do you still… do you still want me?"

Do I want her? Is she kidding me? How the fuck can she not know?

"Yes," I croak. "Jesus Christ, sweetheart. Always."

Her face lights up, so relieved, like there was ever any question, and I can't bear it anymore. I gather her against my chest, burying my face in her hair. She grabs fistfuls of my sweatshirt, pulling me just as close, and I'm burning up from the inside with joy.

"Coach?" someone calls in the background. I check my watch and curse.

"Time! Finish up!"

They grumble loudly, the hiss and whir of the machines fading away, but I don't give a shit. I suck in a lungful of Keeley's shampoo.

"Come with me." I take her hand in mine, heart swelling when she doesn't pull away. I lead her through the warehouse, past lines of curious eyes, all the way to my office at the back of the room. "Take ten!" I call out as I yank open the door, hustling Keeley into the dark room.

The light flicks on, and I wince. A sea of training logs and meal plans cover my desk, along with two empty coffee mugs. My pen pot has fallen over. The rest of my office is not much better either, with every piece of furniture draped in abandoned jackets and piled high with sports equipment.

"So messy," Keeley murmurs, a wicked glint in her eye as she turns to me. I push the door closed and lock it.

"You drove here?" I want to make sense of this. I want to know exactly what led her to the warehouse door.

"Raine drove me. She's gone to a cafe to wait."

My heart sinks, pain lancing through my chest. "You're not staying?"

Keeley cocks her head. "I wasn't sure if you'd want me to."

"Yes." Fuck. "God, yes. Keeley. I never want you out of my sight again."

Her face brightens, even as she backs up to my desk and perches on the edge of it.

"That could be a challenge. Since I still have the summer semester."

"And after that?"

She shrugs. "I could be bargained with."

That's all I need to hear. Wherever she wants to live or work, I'll follow. People need coaches everywhere.

"A semester is a long time."

She hums. "You'll have to come and visit."

"Will you let me in this time?"

She smirks. "You'll have to visit and see."

God. How did I manage nearly two months without her? I thought sending all those letters and never hearing back, I'd go insane. But now she's here, hopping down off my desk and—

And sweeping everything onto the floor. Papers fall in a fluttering landslide as the pen pot clatters against the bare cement.

I bark out a laugh as she turns to me, grinning.

"As good as you hoped?"

"Better." She bites her lip, suddenly shy. "Come here?"

It's not a question. Not for me, at least. There's an unstoppable pull between us. I cross to her, debris crunching under my boots, and lift her back onto the desk then step between her thighs. We're both still wrapped in layers, but when are we not?

Keeley nips at my earlobe.

"You left the job half done, professor."

"What do you…" Her meaning dawns, and I bite back a curse. I slide a hand between us, rubbing the waistband of her leggings between my thumb and forefinger as I lower my head and kiss her hard.

She sighs against my mouth. Wriggles closer; tilts her head; parts her lips and flicks her tongue against mine. It's everything I remembered and more, and heat surges through me as I rock against her core, my hard length only parted from her by a few layers of fabric.

She grabs my wrist, urging me on, and I dip my fingers inside. She's hot and slick, just as ready for me as before.

"Keeley." I press my forehead against hers, rocking it from side to side as I slide one finger through her slit. She moans, her hips arching against me. Urging me on, on, on.

I circle her clit, rubbing her there as her breathing quickens.

But she short-circuits my brain when she says, "Wait, Beckett. I want all of you this time."

I keep rubbing her—no reason she can't have both—but hunger twists inside me and I grow impossibly harder. Yes. Fuck. I want that too.

It's only when she's shaking in my arms, coming apart on my fingers, that cold reality washes over me.

"Shit."

She blinks up at me, bleary. "Did I do something wrong?"

"What? No, of course not. Sweetheart, I don't have a condom." Because why would I have one here? I'm at work, and what's more, I haven't wanted anyone since Keeley. Even the thought turned my stomach.

We'll have to wait. It's—it's fine. What matters is she's here, and I made her come, and—

Keeley pulls a foil packet out of her coat pocket and grins.

"I thought coaches were always prepared?"

"Keeley."

She rolls it onto me with shaking fingers. It's a little clumsy, unpracticed, but it's perfect, she's perfect, and her sharp intake of breath when she really looks at all of me makes me want to beat my chest.

"Think you can handle it?"

"Oh, shut up." But she smiles up at me so sweetly, I could die.

It's... awkward. On the desk. Finding the right height, the right angle. And a knot winds tighter and tighter in my chest—I need to make this good for her.

I need to be good for her.

So when we finally find our rhythm, when I slide deeper and deeper inside her and her gasps turn to moans, relief shudders through me along with triumph. I cup the side of her face, pressing kisses all over her cheeks, and when she drags my bottom lip between her teeth, I groan.

Our shared gasps fill my office. The steady creak of the desk; the wet pump of my cock between her thighs. To an outsider, it might seem crass, but it's the best sound I've ever heard—until Keeley tightens around me, my fingers blurring on her clit as she comes with a tiny squeak.

God.

Definitely need to record that.

I open my mouth to tell her about my plans for a new ringtone—I want to hear her laugh—but the sensations are building too hot, too fast, and there's a tingle at the base of my spine. The orgasm is wrenched out of me, practically turning me inside out as I press my face against her collarbone and groan. It goes on and on, emptying into the condom, and her palms smooth over my shoulders as she whispers in my ear.

About how good it was.

How perfect it feels.

How long she's been waiting for me.

Fuck.

"Sweetheart." I gather her closer against my chest, my cock still wedged inside her. She melts into me, limbs wrapping and holding me close. "Please don't push me away again. I can't bear it."

She snorts, but it's more amused than bitter.

"I won't if you won't."

"Deal."

We stay there well past the end of training. I'll make it up to the team tomorrow, but right now, I can't pretend to be sorry.

I've been waiting for this just as long as she has. Longer, even.

Keeley.

She's perfect. And she's mine.

17

Epilogue

He's here.

Crap.

I thought I had more time. I was going to shower; put on something other than sweaty gym gear; eat something so my stomach stops growling.

I was going to clean the apartment, damn it. Now I've lost the high ground. Beckett's voice drifts into the kitchen as Lucy lets him in, chattering about the last time he visited. His voice is warm, and to anyone else he'd sound laid back. Completely casual.

I can hear the impatient undertone, though. He wants to see me. Now.

Well, he'll get his wish, but it means seeing me in this state. My mouth twists, rueful, as I step out into the living room.

Beckett's face lights up, and it's like the sun peeking through the clouds. It's always the same when he sees me. It doesn't matter if he saw me ten days or ten minutes ago—if I'm in front of him or on a video call.

A girl could get used to someone looking at her like that. Like the center of his universe. I bounce over and wrap my arms around his neck, sweaty gym clothes and all.

"Sweetheart." He smirks at me as I rock back on my heels. "You dressed up for me? You shouldn't have."

I toss my tangled hair over my shoulder. "I know you like me all gross."

"You guys are weird," Raine murmurs as she walks past. She crosses to the sofa, flopping down next to Lucy and Gideon and flicking through the TV channels. If it bothers her to have two ex-professors hanging around, she doesn't say anything.

But then, Raine is hard to read.

"Two down." I drag Beckett across the room, perching on the arm of the sofa and nudging Raine's shoulder. "Which professor are you going to ruin?"

Raine's mouth curls, and a tiny shiver runs down my spine. She can be kind of scary.

"I haven't chosen a victim just yet."

We're joking—at least, I'm pretty sure we are—but Gideon gives Beckett a look. Then he bites his lip and the two men burst out laughing.

"What?" Lucy cranes her head to look at Gideon. "What's so funny?"

"Nothing," Beckett snickers. "We've just got a victim in mind." He tugs on my ponytail, winding my hair around his fingers.

"Who?" Raine glances between them, a small crease in her forehead. They both shake their heads, grinning, and she huffs. "Please. It's not like I'd actually do it. Unlike some hussies around here, I don't go seducing my professors."

"You should try it," Lucy chirps.

"Yep." I elbow Beckett. "Ten out of ten. Would recommend."

"I'm not sure I like this," I hear Gideon say.

113

Raine rolls her eyes, flicking through the TV channels, and Beckett tugs me to my feet. He leads me to my bedroom door, eyes hot as they rake over my body.

He ducks his head and murmurs in my ear. "Are you toying with me, sweetheart? Keeping me waiting?"

"Nope." I bump past him, shoving my bedroom door open. I've never been good at making either of us wait. And Beckett's last visit was eight whole days ago.

We have a lot of catching up to do.

THE END

Thanks for reading Bonus Study! I hope it gave you all the best student/professor feelings. & If you enjoyed it, please consider leaving a review!

Have you read Gideon and Lucy's story? Before you do, check out *Off Campus*, a prequel short story about the smokin' hot night they met. Download your free copy here: https://Book Hip.com/GQCNFH

And for more student/professor goodness, check out the next book in the *Office Hours* trilogy: *After Class*.

Kayla xx

Teaser: After Class

"Wouldn't it be hilarious if Raine and Fraser got together?"

Lucy and Keeley chatter loudly as we walk through the rain-slicked city streets, hopping over puddles that glow orange with lamplight. I trail behind, hands in my jacket pockets, no hint of emotion on my face.

Gideon and Beckett laugh too, walking two steps behind me, but more nervously than the girls. The two ex-professors are both devoted to their girlfriends, but there's no denying they gave up a lot for them. Neither of them teach any more, with Gideon working as a writer and critic and Beckett working hours away up the coast to coach an elite rowing team. He drives back down every weekend to spend time with Keeley, and spends most weeknights talking to her on the phone.

No one could blame them for not wanting that for their friend.

To an outsider, they lost out. Gave up esteemed careers as professors to quickly sidestep into other jobs. And the rumors swirled behind them on campus—baseless rumors about sleeping with tons of students and abusing their power.

None of those are true. Obviously. Any idiot can look at these two men and see they fell in love. Gideon is hypnotized by Lucy, staring at her walking ahead of him like he still can't believe she's real. And Beckett is almost painfully tender with Keeley, treasuring her like she's the center of his universe.

I guess I wouldn't mind some of that. Someone worshiping the ground I walk on. I'm only human.

But something tells me it won't come from some dusty old professor. In all honesty, I'm not even sure I'm capable of those things anyway.

Attraction.

Desire.

Feeling such strong emotions for someone that I can't keep away—and inspiring those same feelings in someone else.

Let's just say that I've had a very peaceful college experience so far. I've tried hook-ups, sure. As a personal experiment more than anything. And they were okay, but not worth the awkwardness. And though I've heard plenty about this Fraser—even looked up his staff profile online—I can't picture it.

He seems stuffy. Boring. Cold.

Nothing like the man I'd need to bring me to life. To wake up all the latent feelings and desires that I'm only half-sure are in there somewhere. A big part of me wonders whether it's even real for anyone else, or if they're all exaggerating too to fit in.

But then Beckett comes to visit, and Keeley's walls are thin. So I know it's real.

I suppose tonight is an experiment of sorts. I hop over a puddle, cheered by the thought. It's spring in the city, which means wet and breezy with flashes of pale sunshine in the day. And in the nights like these, it might as well still be winter. I burrow my chin into my jacket collar and tune out the girls' chatter.

We're meeting for drinks to celebrate Gideon's book deal, but I know Lucy and Keeley are both hoping the last professor and I will feel a spark.

Fraser Drummond is a psychology professor. One of the big names in my department. But he's never taught me—he's on some weird sabbatical as a guidance counselor—so I've never really seen him up close.

I seriously doubt he can solve my attraction problem. But maybe he can give me some academic answers. Point me towards some helpful research papers or something.

Maybe Fraser Drummond can set me a private assignment.

* * *

Professor Drummond is... kind of rude.

Not outright. He doesn't say anything brash or insulting; he doesn't sneer or roll his eyes. But when we slide one by one into the booth at the bar, and our eyes meet across the table, he nods once and looks away. He turns to the conversation happening between Keeley and Gideon, her bright stream of questions about his book, and I can practically see Fraser tuning me out. Putting up invisible walls.

Dismissed. Just like that.

I haven't even asked him yet about the psychology of attraction.

I peer at him with narrowed eyes, examining him openly across the booth table. The professor has thick coppery hair and piercing blue eyes, and pale, clean-shaven skin. He's so pale, he looks ghostly. If my mother saw him, she'd chase him outside and tell him to get some sun. At first glance, he seems slender, but only because he's sat next to Beckett. When I look at him, *really* look, I realize his shoulders are broad. Toned.

I scowl down at my whisky and take a sip. He glances over, his eyes ghosting over my drink before he looks away.

Nothing. Not a flicker of emotion or reaction. This man is infuriating.

The whisky spreads over my tongue, smoky and delicious, and I lick a bead of moisture off my top lip. The slightest frown creases his forehead, but he stays fixated on Gideon, his grip tight on his beer bottle.

Fine. Whatever. I don't want to talk to a rude asshole anyway.

"Fraser, how's the study going?"

Apparently Lucy knows him well enough. I perk up, straining to hear his low voice over the din of the bar.

He shrugs and offers her a small smile. "I've paused my research activities."

I sink back against the seat, disappointed. If I were a psychology professor, you'd better believe I'd be heading up studies. Starting projects and focus groups; researching the mysteries of the human brain.

This guy doesn't know how lucky he is.

"Raine's a psychology major." Lucy nods at me, a wicked glint in her eye. "You two should have loads to talk about."

The professor glances at me, his eyes sliding away as quickly as they came. Another shrug.

Asshole.

"I don't teach any more."

"Why not?" I blurt out. He looks at me again, the movement sharp. I glare back. This grumpy ghost of a man doesn't intimidate me.

He opens his mouth to answer, but then closes it again. Something stirs deep in his eyes, something troubled and panicked, but then Beckett swoops to his rescue.

"Fraser's a do-gooder." He claps his friend on the shoulder. "He's too busy saving troubled souls as a guidance counselor."

That's not it, I want to scream, but apparently no one else can see it—the haunted look in this man's eyes. They all nod and smile and talk about how good he is, how giving, and can't they see that they're making it worse? His face drains impossibly paler, almost gray, and he swallows hard as he forces a smile.

When his gaze lands on me again, he jerks back slightly. I'm scowling at him, trying to pick through his secrets. If I could, I'd reach over and tilt his head to the side, cupping my hand beneath his ear as those secrets dripped glittering into my palm.

His eyes narrow, his expression darkening, those icy eyes still fixed on mine, and something coils in my abdomen. Something hot and aching.

Oh.

I press my thighs together, shifting on my seat, never breaking the eye contact between us. Somehow he reads that motion too, something knowing and almost cruel in the way he watches me, and my skin flushes to a thousand degrees. I want to catalogue these sensations. Make a bullet pointed list so that I can compare them to the academic notes on attraction on my laptop.

There's the hollow, aching feeling in my core, twisting tighter with every breath, and the way my pulse thrums faster under my skin. Colors are brighter; every sound and smell is heightened, and god, what does this man smell like? I need to know.

I swipe my whisky glass off the table with a trembling hand. It burns the back of my throat, anchoring me back to reality. And when I place the glass back down with a thud, he finally, *finally,* looks away.

My breath leaves my chest. I wilt back against the leather seats.

I feel like I've just done one of Keeley's horrible work outs.

This is it. This is perfect! I sit up ramrod straight, my mind racing as I tune out the conversation. Sure, he's rude and standoffish, clearly damaged in some way, but that's not the point. Professor Fraser Drummond makes me *feel*.

Surely he won't refuse to help me explore these sensations. Even just academically.

You know. For science.

About the Author

Kayla Wren is a British author who writes steamy New Adult romance. She loves Reverse Harem, Enemies-to-Lovers, and Forbidden Love tropes.

Kayla writes prickly men with hearts of gold, secretly-sexy geeks, and—best of all—she's ALWAYS had a thing for the villains.

You can connect with me on:

- https://www.kaylawrenauthor.com
- https://www.facebook.com/kaylawrenauthor
- https://www.bookbub.com/authors/kayla-wren

Subscribe to my newsletter:

- https://www.kaylawrenauthor.com/newsletter

Also by Kayla Wren

Year of the Harem Collection:
Lords of Summer
Autumn Tricksters
Knights of Winter
Spring Kings

Standalone titles:
The Naughty List

www.ingramcontent.com/pod-product-compliance
Lightning Source LLC
Chambersburg PA
CBHW030542130626
46552CB00006B/2383

* 9 7 8 1 9 1 4 2 4 2 3 6 6 *